BULLETPROOF SUZY

Bulletproof Suzy

Ian Brotherhood

MYRMIDON

Myrmidon Books Ltd
Rotterdam House
116 Quayside
Newcastle upon Tyne
NE1 3DY
www.myrmidonbooks.com

Published by Myrmidon 2006

A catalogue record for this book is available from the British Library.

ISBN 978-1-905802-00-5 Hardback
ISBN 978-1-905802-01-2 Trade Paperback

Set in 11.5/14.5pt Sabon by
Falcon Oast Graphic Arts Limited, East Hoathly, East Sussex

Printed and bound in Great Britain
by Mackays of Chatham, Chatham, Kent

A&JRULEOK

OLRATW
WWWHBAG
ANWBAH
ECTTWW
BWWTFMC
WLBAC
IWWDAWWK
ATWMTST

IDMLP98

L&P2ALL

IBJUL06

BULLETPROOF SUZY

CHAPTER ONE

~ You up for this or not then? I say.

It's hard to pinpoint exactly when something starts. Tracing back, where do you stop? But that night seems as good a point as any. Maybe it should start the night before, when a knife slices through my best friend's left eyeball, but that's where it all stopped for Joanne. The next night is where it, or this, starts for me, and where I choose to start it for you. If you are up for it, that is.

So it's after tea and, what with clocks just about to be set back so that we're into twilight-zone time again, it's unusually dark, and everyone would be a bit tetchy and out of sorts I suppose anyway. I've already laid out the case, made it as simple as I can, but the girls aren't happy. That's Danny's fault. She's getting to them, giving them second thoughts. Not doubts as such, but certainly thoughts, and you don't want that when you're talking about giving someone the ultimate doing, as I most surely am.

~ It wasn't us did Joanne, but if we hammer Shuggs

it'll be us end up slammed inside, that's for sure, says Danny, and with that tone of pure defiance I've noted plenty times lately, and bolder and surlier with every time I should add.

She's ashy-coloured, kind of dusty and fearful of complexion, but when someone goes dusty and ashy and is seemingly fearful, you should always be aware that this may be not only because of fear, but because of a build-up of intention, trepidation regarding one's own plans. So maybe young Miss Danny is planning to do something fearful to me, at least, that's the feeling I suddenly get, and so I make my way across to the window, turning away from her as I ponder action immediate-wise. I pull the curtains further apart and take a half-hearted squint out at the view. The rain stopped, I can see all the way down to the river, and that's four miles at least, and further on again down the estuary I can make out the lights slung along the big bridge. That's twenty miles. It's the best thing about living up so high.

~ If we don't get him, I say, still staring at the twinkly lights of the airport, no one else will.

Even though it's still cloudy overhead, the cloud so close that it's tinged orange by the streetlights and the aircraft warning block-lights, I can see pure black sky away over by the hills past the river, and in this patch of blackness I can make out sparkles of scattered stars, and the tingling of these few stars is almost as bright as the lights on the plane landing at the airport, and I try to figure how that can be, trying to get my mind off Danny and her mutinous tone.

~ It's not like she was really one of us anyway, continues Danny, and the stars take on the same red splinters that are coming from the lights on the plane, and the cloud seems suddenly to shift down and covers the hills and the river, and it's almost as if that's Danny's fault.

~ Stuck-up bitch spent half her time in that library, didn't want to know anyone, wouldn't give us the time of day, that's for sure, says Danny, and she's still checking her hair in the mirror.

I imagine a mug-full of mercury in my belly, way down in my belly, in between my hips. That has to be still, no ripples, before you start throwing any weight about. That's what I was taught, so I still do it, even if it's only for half of a second. So that's still and smooth, no ripples. Check the others.

Kelly's perched on the end of my bed, leaning on her knees, grimacing at the carpet. Gerry is looking at me but nodding without smile in apparent agreement with Danny, who's now turned to face my dressing table mirror, and she fiddles about with her earring and is pulling a tissue from my box when I crack her one. It's not a proper punch as such, more of a slap on the back of her head, but she gets a fright and sort of yelps and cowers away for a half-snatch before turning fast with her right coming up, fingers splayed and claw-like. I jerk back, and toy with throwing a kick, but the dresser will be wrecked with solid Danny landing atop it so move back instead and let the heavy one up to do what she will, and her nails flash across my face, a tad close for the proverbial, so out with the right and a fistful of hair, jerk and turn like a matadoress, if there be such a thing, and let the heavy-boned Danny pass below my outstretched arm, grab her collar with free left as she lumbers through, moderately forceful left knee to kidney-land and Danny's knees meet the carpet. Very easy now, so gentle shoulder-push, legs akimbo, down we go on the barrel-chest, one hand at windpipe, little squeeze, other hand snaps out two fingers to gently place tips at base of those big brown peepers, then slowly push just below the lower lids so white shows and she breathes hard, and a thin line of greyish snot is stringing and swinging across her lips.

~ Last chance, Danny, I say, and my voice has a deep wobble, like I have to clear my throat. I'm having Shuggs fair or foul, like it or not. So, last time of last times, you up for this or not?

My own eyes water and widen, but I'm so quiet, just like a wee mouse, a wee tiny mouse with a dry mouth and twingling belly. Danny's rigid and white but she shakes out a tiny nod, not wanting to push her eyeballs any further onto my fingernails. I draw my hand back, then she blinks a couple of times and those big brown peepers go sort of soft and backing-down, giving it okay, enough.

~ Sorry, Suzy. You're right, you're right, she says, sounding properly contrite.

I get up, and now it's my turn to fix my hair, not that it takes a lot of fixing at this time – straight and half-blonde, half-brown thanks to a previous bleach-job I've been growing-out, and about as uninteresting as any head of hair can be – my fingers are adept at gathering and twisting with the band to keep it all away out of my face in a pony-tail which only just brushes the ticklish nape, tell-tale sign that it's overdue a decent cut. I'm a bit heavier now, but then was at my proper fighting weight of ten-eleven, and little of that was fat. Doesn't look that heavy on paper, and I'm almost five-six. Yeah, I was in good shape. Suzy, I'm called, and Danny and Kelly and Gerry are my little ladies.

To the Viewhill locals I'm Bulletproof Suzy, but don't ask me where that comes from. I've never been shot at, well not then anyroad, so it's hard to see the origin, but I suppose it's meant as a compliment of sorts, and can be taken as such if you are a female, such as I am, who does not seek to cultivate a butter-wouldn't-melt image among her peers. That's not to say I much like it all the same. I can take it from strangers, as they don't know any better, but not from my little ladies or anyone else in Magenta, that being our block.

More to the point, my name isn't Suzy or Suzanne. My name is Francine. Francine Brallahan. It should really be Francine MacLeod-Brallahan if Mum's to be given her place. And if you want to get really finicky, as might happen if required to complete an application for a passport or somesuch similarly serious document, I should really be writing Marianne Francine Kylie Brallahan. The further complication, which only ever arises should the procedure involve historical documents, or maybe if you were the sort to like raking about in family related stuff such as ancestral trees and suchlike, is that when my great granda came over from Ireland he was using the spelling that was a direct translation of his Gaelic name, so that was full of gees and aiches that you don't say. Even Mum dropped the 'O'. Anyway, it has to be admitted, much as I like my own real name, that Francine O'Brallahan doesn't really suit the work I'm doing, so it's as well to ditch it for now.

*

I tuck my white shirt back into the leggings and smooth down the front. Danny certainly hasn't done any damage, but I look somewhat dishevelled and a bit flushed. I've always hated that flushed look as it gives me a bloated and anxious appearance which does not necessarily reflect the way I feel.

Although I take my physique from my Dad – God rest the poxy fuck – my face is all Mum's, all fair skin from Norway or Finland or somesuch cold bastard of a place, cheek-bones you could open envelopes with and teeth a wee bit too big for my gob, straight and white though they are. There's an Irish singer who looks very much like me at that point, a lass with some cred and much success, but it saddens me to say that I think her stuff is shite so I don't gush enthusiasm at any comparison. Still, I must be a bit of a sight whatever way you choose to look at me.

Now, Joanne – there was the girl with the looks. The girl who starts this argument now between me and Danny, the girl who they've found dead at the foot of Magenta not twenty-four hours ago, and certainly the person who I would pick first of all out of everyone in the world as my best friend ever.

Kelly goes all sort of quiet and withdrawn, interested in anything but me or Danny now that the brief set-to has been and gone and I see her sort of tensing up as I cross to where she has let herself half-lie on the bed, but her knees are drawn up by way of protection and even if she is trying to look laid-back and relaxed, she looks not a jot comfortable and knows I know it.

~ Alright, Kelly dear? I enquire, smiling, and the tone alerts her.

She looks up slow, blue eyes tight and small-holed, like she's expecting a slap.

~ Yeah, Suzy, fine, she says, trying to stay cool, doing not a bad job voice-wise.

~ Just before our little tetatet there I thought I caught something of a contribution from your good self. Anything further to add? I ask.

She shakes her head, chin sticking out, but glancing over at Danny, who has now clambered back onto the dressing-table chair and is massaging her red neck.

~ Speak up then, I say.

~ Nothing further to add, Kelly says low and mild.

~ That's the gemm, doll, I say, and sit beside her on the end of my bed.

She shifts up a wee bit to give me room, and stares down at the floor again, face cupped in hands. She's breathing heavily, maybe angry. I adjust her collar a little where it's folded back. The 'Piper' label is showing. Real class material, must've cost a ton and a half easy. She's a smartish dresser is our Kelly, ever bleeding her old dearests for the latest arrivals at The Depot and the best looking of us if you like magazine style.

Strange as it maybe seems, I think I'm even more wary of Kelly than Danny. Danny, as I have indicated, is something of a heavyweight, and although she is a very powerful young lady and can press almost a quarter as much again as my good self, I've a sneaking feeling that she's maybe partaken of a few cowbloaters in her time, and this short-termist approach to muscular development has taken it's toll in terms of her speed and general alertness. Kelly, by contrast, is the runt of the outfit, at about seven and a half sad stone, arms like wee skinny stickbags, and pipe-cleaner fingers. Her legs are quite long for her height but she appears so slight and delicate that it's hard to imagine that she has actually killed – the wee psycho bastard has a temper off the scale altogether. Still, it's usually when she's on something that she gets going, so as long as we keep her away from the schnapps Blinders and don't let her drop anything into an empty belly, she's quiet and safe enough and most handy when things get physical.

Now it's getting on. Half seven, already dark, and still not a bit of work done. Joanne's murder has thrown everything into confusion, but the work goes on regardless, tough as it may be. Danny's mouthing off is, I'm quite sure, more to do with fear of reprisal and possible rozzer-entanglement than any desire to take advantage of me in my weakened state, but giving her that slap won't have done any harm as far as re-affirming my status is concerned. And this is surely one of those times you read about in management manuals and all that, when all those about you are losing their heads etc.

Not that my little ladies appear to be losing it at all. I know that it's me who's hurting the most, and I know that they know that I can't show it. Not yet. It would be easy to go to town on Danny, possibly perhaps even take the three of them on and kick some of my pain into them. But no good can come of that. I want Shuggs and his merry men, and I want to do it properly. And for that I need my little ladies about me and behind me and with me. The only way to do that now is to get them back to work, where we look out for each other regardless.

Danny has resumed playing with her dodgy earring, which provides a good excuse not to have to look in my general direction. Kelly sits up, reaches over to take a tissue from my box and starts blowing her beak into it. Kelly's nose is always running. Gerry always says that Kelly's nose is running and her feet are smelling so that means she must be upside-down, and Kelly always tuts at that and Danny always laughs her big madman's laugh and I always keep a straight face even though I want to smile. Gerry hasn't moved a muscle since she came in, still sat on the chair by the window, picking at her fingernails and dreaming. She's likely thinking about her slob of a boyfriend who she's been with the night before and it seems that they may have had words 'cos she's sort of gloomy of face and quiet like she's pondering what might happen as well as what already has.

~ Ladies, the night is young, I say.

I like that intro, theatrical and a tad naff as it is, it serves as a sort of amber light for the girls, and when they know that work is about to begin their attention sparks up. Gerry leaves her nails alone and looks up, Kelly takes a final, rattling sniff, and Danny swivels around on the dressing table chair, gently rubbing a slightly reddened eyelid.

~ Now I know it's a touchy subject, and dearest Miss Danny just demonstrated the depth of her feelings about it all, but plain fact is that what happened to Joanne happened right down there on our doorstep. If we're not very careful it might be one of us next, so I want to stress to you again that we have to stick together whether we like it or not. Shuggs and his boys have taken a good few poundings off us in the last wee while, but what they did here was evil. I know we never saw Joanne for a while. And she wasn't one of us, as Danny pointed out. I'll give you that. But she went to the same school as me, was in the same year. You know I wanted her in with us, offered her a place. She could've done it no problem. But she had her wee job in the library. We can't look down on her for that. It was a crappy, arse-burster of a shift but she took it and wanted it, worked seventy hours a week trying to give herself a decent start. That's the whole point here. Joanne was trying to get on the way we've been told by the coupons and suits since knee-high, the only way that can get you out of this hole. Stay at school, get the papers, grab a crappy starter and move on up. That's the way she chose, and what does it get her? Gets her filleted like a fucking fish, that's what.

Danny holds my stare. She's unscrewing the lid of her lipstick, rubbing a little of the oil between her fingers. Gerry coughs, Kelly sniffs. No tears anywhere, but I can feel my eyeballs giving it tingle, and have to take a real deep breath. Gerry suddenly pipes up with her very first words since arriving an hour or more ago.

~ She never even got a chance to fight back, she says with genuine gloom, Josie says she never had a chance.

Exactly what slobboid boyfriend Josie knows about it all is beyond me, but we shall surely find out in due course.

~ None of us needs reminding that plenty of teams are wanting into Viewhill, and there's those among them with guns and what-not. But they don't know the place. We do, and as long as we keep our wits about us there's no reason we can't keep them out. Shuggs is going way out of his depth. So don't listen to the rabbit-gobs in the pee-oh, and don't start freaking when you hear old faces gassing on about the Ruck team and Easter krewes. Right? Just keep the heid. Stick together. Right? Business as normal ladies. For now anyroad.

I'm not even sure they're listening, and not sure what I'm saying, but my little ladies nod, sad and weak, as if the night's already over and they've done a full shift.

~ Right?! I yell.

~ Right! they shout in reply, but a tad droopy.

Time to get them out for some fresh air.

I keep an eye on Danny as we wait for the lift to show, twenty-three up, top dancer of all. It can take a while for the box to get here, so the girls stand chatting and I think about Joanne lying there way below, day before, cut and dead and cold, and up above us the big darkening sky will be further away when we get down to ground floor, and just as dark. It's not too windy tonight, 'cos we're not swaying. Even when it gets bad with the wind coming from the sea, the water moves in the bog pan and the fish in the tank maybe think they've been set loose into the big real sea, but even as bad as that we don't notice so much, we just sway with it, like high-rise crows-nesters. It takes a while to get used to it. Something to do with liquid in our earholes, or so I've heard.

Waiting for the box to arrive, I can see Danny watching me in the reflection on the steel of the box doors. We look good, as usual, all clean and hair nice, Gerry caked with make-up as is her style, but us others plain apart from perhaps just a touch of lippy. Have to keep appearances up, try to look professional. This is surely what it's all about, why it happened, at least in part. The money. Always the money.

We've fallen behind a bit of late, so tonight, right now, is as good a time as any to crack on and get back on an even keel. The night has only started, and if we don't dilly and dally and get distracted, we might cover some ground. Not that there's even any real chance of being distracted by sight of Shuggs – gallus and gemmy as he undoubtedly is, he's never been that daft. There's plenty of other folk with much bigger axes to grind than us, but I know in my head and my heart that if I get my hands on him he won't have a hope.

I'm still admiring us in the shiny steel when we hear the guts of the thing croaking and grinding and pulling cables and clunking to an unhealthy-sounding stop – the doors part right where me and Danny are staring at each other like two deformities in a circus mirror-hall, twisted heads and loopy mad limbs.

We go straight to The Hall, and it's very quiet for a Thursday. Usually there's the Pinkstons and the Sights and the Hills, the MacNamaras and the Johnsons, in varying numbers, but camped in their usual alcoves with friends all about. Other families come down too, but the aforementioned are the biggest and most regular clans, and if strangers or smaller squads are using the tables, Declan the boss will ask them to make space, and have them ejected if they do not comply with a good grace. The Hall is the only pool lounge left where we know there's no chance of unexpected nonsense, as all the regulars are Magenta residents and no Cerulean campers are admitted on the grounds that the inevitable tension ruins the cordial, if boisterous atmosphere. So we're always made very welcome, and our favoured patch, up at the end of the main pool room by the fire exit, is seldom occupied.

The Pinkstons are an especially hospitable crowd, there being twenty or more of them in the one family, and not one a bad egg. They occupy the whole of Magenta's sixteenth floor.

Granda Pink, or Gramps as known to all, is actually Dad to most of them and he's a straight-up sort. He's a youngish sixty, still fit, and numerous tales tell of his prowess with a snooker cue. Maybe he was on the telly once, or won some competition, but he doesn't talk about it anyway, modest sort that he is. And I know for sure that Granda Pink is not above using cues to settle arguments and such when the need arises, and he can scrap with the best of them. And so, by and large, his brood is safe from the attentions of Shuggs and the other Cherries. I suppose Gramps Pink is held up by many of my Magenta neighbours as a sort of resident wise old bloke sort, and is much asked for favours, perhaps as often as I am myself. And Gramps knows that we are useful to him, with the vice-versa rule applying also, and he does give us a nod now and then if he hears that the Cherries are after someone or other in particular. Likewise, we know many friends and acquaintances of the various Pinkstons, and tip them in advance if there is a job pending imminently on such and such a family member's head, or perhaps that of an associate.

So my little ladies advance to our table, which is itself a wee bit raised up on a sort of platform arrangement so we can get a good scan at what's happening at the other tables as well as keep half an eyeball directed out the window simultaneous-wise. Not that a night streetscape on Viewhill's edge offers much by way of visuals, despite the name bestowed on the area by someone who obviously thought otherwise, or perhaps named it in a different time, when there was indeed something to see. There might be a set-to among the local up-and-comers from time to time, or now and then a chase with the rozzlings speeding after nerrdowells in the safety of their Kalibros, but for the most part the orange-lit broad line which is the street stays bare, more often than not shining with fresh rain

The barperson, who must be a new character by my reckoning, has already poured three of the four half-Flashes which start the evening. I'm about to interrogate him as regards his apparent powers of telepathy when Gramps Pink emerges from the Gentleman's powder room, smiling his big gappy smile and looking decidedly excited.

~ Suzy babe, he growls in slabberish style, just the very girl I'm after.

Gramps is yet another of the male species who has that kind of shininess about the eyes when he looks at you, always stealing a sly glance at one's nether regions and other erogenous zones, and moving his tongue about. But he's nice with it, and I tend to feel almost sorry for him as I'm pretty sure he doesn't particularly like the idea of being seen ogling a mere eighteen year old. But at least there's a kind of honesty about him, so he doesn't even try to conceal it. So I smile one of my girly smiles and point at the drinks which the new lad has by now decorated with thick lime quarters and coloured ice balls. Gramps makes a half-bow, all chivalrous and don't-mention-it-at-all.

~ What's a double-brace of half-Flashes for a squad as

delectable as Suzy's? he gushes, but almost right away his smile sort of droops and falls off and he backs away and beckons me to join him on the two-seater just by the puggie machines.

He's all conspiratorial and eyebrows ahop as we get a seat, and he takes a very serious sook at his long whisky before he speaks.

~ Here, Suzy, you girls come down by the Cherry basket tonight? he asks, and I shake my head the once.

~ Bit late off the mark tonight, Gramps, I say, and he has a quick scan about the place, and even though there's no-one in he doesn't know, he peers hard at the door at the head of the stairs, as if perhaps he's expecting someone to enter at any moment, and from the expression on the old grumpy wrinkly bag-eyed face it seems that the prospect of this person, whoever it might be, coming into The Hall, is something that does not amuse or reassure him in any way.

In fact, in the pause which lasts a few seconds I'm pretty sure that Gramps is positively scared, or if not scared, at least so excited and jumpy that I would surely ascribe his nervousness to the use of restricted substances if I knew not that he's a man with very strong feelings about some drugs, and would never partake of the trendier concoctions. He sits further back in his seat so that from the entrance he cannot now be seen, obscured as he is by the side of the virtual-golf machine. There's a few of the Sights up at the bar, but they're well away, one asleep on folded arms, the other two swapping slurs and dribbles by way of conversation. No danger of anyone hearing. He takes a deep breath and another long pull at the whisky.

~ That girl that got done. You knew her right? he says

23

rather than asks, and I nod and try to look composed.

He stabs a big fat red finger on the table top, and there's a sort of shakiness in his voice.

~ Pure unbelievable by the way. Our Harry was there just after. Says he never saw the likes.

I want to stop Gramps then. It seems that everyone and their pets saw Joanne being killed, and I'm maybe one of the few people in the whole world who would have tried to help, maybe even the only one who really could have helped and I was ten minutes away, on a fucking bus dreaming about taking a holiday, picking at my nail varnish, smelling the hairspray of the old dear sat afront me as Joanne was bleeding to death outside my own house. So I want to stop Gramps but I know that he's sort of old-school when it comes to talking about gore and violence and such in front of women, even if it is me he's talking to, and he won't lay it on too thick, so I let him go on.

~ Now I know you and Shuggs are not bosom buddies. And I know you'll think he had something to do with it. That's the gas right now. But I can tell you, Suzy, I can tell you for fact it wasn't him. He was there alright, Shuggs and his rent-boy shower of scumbag pals. But they shat it big-style, ended up beating a retreat into the Cherry basket before Joanne was even knifed. That's what Harry tells me. He knows what he's talking about, Suzy. And what he says is that it was some Southside crew.

I sort of freeze I suppose, just for a moment feeling that the old hearing must be going. Southsiders in Viewhill? Oh heavens no. Dearie me, no. That's like green men coming from Mars, or a cheesy moon. Some things do not happen. But Gramps is not given to flights of fancy, and neither is eldest son Harry, who has spent more than half of his forty years inside the big biscuit tin, and knows better than most the structure and behaviour of the urban teams.

I struggle to recall any names I might've heard over past years. They are the stuff of half-stories, these dodgy legends that come to friends via unnamed others, and can usually be safely ignored. People who are larger than fictional characters, who have names and physiques and move in circumstances that defy belief, and rightly so. But there are some who exist, who have been seen and heard and occasionally felt. They have names.

~ The Flannagans?

Gramps shakes his big jowly whisky-soaked face then, and clatters his teeth together as if the name itself is actually rattling about in his gob.

~ The Grays?

He makes a sound like a cat coughing, and a half-melted ice-ball shoots from his trap across the table. He clears his throat and shakes his big head at the same time. The only other name is one I hesitate to even think.

~ The Shaws? I say.

Gramps Pink slaps the table, and accidentally sends the red tin ashtray spinning across the formica top. I slap my fingers on its edge just as it's about to tipple carpetward. My guts turn upside, down and sidey-ways, all fucking ways, mercury slopping and folding over on itself. The Shaws? Here?

The room starts to move, as if Gramps is part of a big film screen and someone is pulling the whole thing about as I try to watch. Up and across. I mumble something about excusing me for a minute to Gramps and he replies but I don't hear it.

I have to get to the bog as fast as I can 'cos my knees are becoming some sort of soft confectionery-type jelly material and I get into the cubicle, drop down to my new jelly knees and I grasp the toilet bowl to keep the fucker still and I throw up and honk and honk and throw up until I can neither throw up nor honk any more.

CHAPTER TWO

Of course I've heard of them. Everyone has. The Shaws at that time are the best known team in the town, never out of the papers what with a few murders, at least three of them in this past year or so, and no end of fires and robberies and battles with the rozzoids at all times of day and night.

But what in the bluest of blue blazes are they doing up this neck of the proverbials? It's a miracle they got over the river at all, never mind as far up as here, and what they did to Joanne was pure evil. Why her?

Gramps Pink must've sussed that the information has hit me rather hard 'cos when I get back from the Ladies he's at the bar alone, and he beckons me close.

~ Listen, Suzy, he gruffs, and fairly damp of eye unless I'm much mistaken, I don't know exactly what happened, but you'd best watch your back pal. You and your girls. That's a big team turned up at your patch last night, and any squad mad enough to do what they did to that poor lass has to have a grade-A fucker at the helm, so you mind yourself, you hear? You give me a shout you need a hand. Right?

So I thank Gramps Pink, and I shake his hand, then he helps me back to our corner with the drinks. He stands for a minute or three and has a word with my little ladies, all niceties, no mention of Shaws or Joanne. Then he plods back over to where a couple of his sons are playing dominos. I stay put, wiping the condensation off the glass, feeling removed from it all, and it's Danny has to tap my arm to kind of drag me back to the here and now as it were.

~ What's that all about then? she asks, not unreasonably I suppose.

I take a tentative sip at the half-Flash. Rancid bastard cider – it always takes me a couple to kill the taste.

~ Nothing, Danny, sweetness, I reply, but I can feel her eyes searching my face for a clue.

I pull out my book and little pen and allow the others to get on with their game as I check the computer print-out for who's still outstanding, who might be good for an advance on their next month, and who is due a share of whatever heaviness is fated to transpire as the night progresses. But my eyes glide over the names and addresses and amounts, not really taking them in at all. I keep seeing Joanne's face, her blood spread over the orange pavement, the rozzlings pulling great long ribbony tapes around the lamp-posts, and her eyes, one closed, the other gone.

So it wasn't Shuggs? In a way I feel annoyed that the wee shagger is off the hook. I want it to be him, and the fact that it isn't makes things ever more complicated. Up until five minutes ago it was simple, the next step seemed clear, and revenge would be possible. But now?

No-one springs to mind. Joanne had no enemies that I know of. Everyone liked her. Maybe that was what was infuriating about her sometimes. She was so nice. Too nice. No-one could be as nice as that without there being some major catch, like she had to be a maddie by night or was into torturing kittens and puppies in secret.

But I know she was as nice as she appeared to be. If she wasn't so bloody nice we might never have split, and she might still be alive. I make myself stop thinking about her cos I'll surely start gushing right here and now. Look at the figures, the names, the flat numbers. Concentrate on work, 'cos you'll throw it all away if you don't. It's close to falling apart. Don't let it. She always hated it, told you not to. But you did, and you mustn't chuck it now, no matter how hard. If you don't do it, someone else will. Like Danny.

It's been getting harder of late to get the dosh in. At first it was easy-street. The money's still there in the bank, and I'm almost halfway to my target, but I thought a year would be long enough to hit twenty grand and that's proving to have been a bit of chicken-counting on my part. I'm at the eleven mark and managing very nicely it has to be said, making all sorts of plans to get myself off to Spain or maybe Italy or France, some-where a good bit away where I can walk down the street and not be hassled and have to watch my back non-stop.

It must be well over a year ago me and Joanne were in the Job Shop doing the usual aimless wander-about prior to the actual signing, and she's moaning her head off about how she can't stand it any more, how she has to get something, even if it turns out just to be some shitey waitress-type arrangement, or maybe even one of those warehouses where everyone's connected to a phone being nice to total strangers. So I'm a tad sarky with her and encouraging her to do that 'cos if there's anyone who can be nice to total strangers it is surely her nice self and she goes in a huffy mood and gives it her usual spiel about manners costing zilch and so on, and a lecture into the bargain about sarcasm being the lowest form of wit etc., which puts me in a huff and we end up sort of walking about with each other but not talking, and it's a bit daft but par for the course at that time what with general money worries affecting us both in our own ways.

So we sign and we head off again, and it's an August day, not that sunny but still warm enough to be clammy and a bit like oppressive, what with slate-grey clouds kind of hovering about and a white disc of sun trying to steam them all away but having no joy. So I say how about taking a wee donner up town, maybe stagger about the shops and see what can be blagged music-wise, and she's game for that so off we plod, sauntering as is our style.

The road into town seems dead quiet pedestrian-wise that day on account of there being traffic build-ups, and it is amusing to watch folk bursting out of their wee road-bound ovens in the heat, peering into the distance to try and locate the end of the cars, shouting at each other inside and honking their horns at the god of traffic jams, but it's not until we get into the heart of the city that we realise why these snarl-ups are happening.

~ It's the demo, explains Joanne, and I have no

reason to doubt it seeing as how she keeps up with things political and radical and so forth, being interested in all that sort of gumph.

~ It's the rates hikes.

These hikes she refers to are the council tax rises, most unwelcome by all, but not so much of a bother for me and her directly what with us being signers who earn not a penny, and thus are not forced to pay much more than next to zero.

~ Come and we'll go in, says Joanne.

So I'm not that keen at all. It's warm enough to be uncomfy and I'd rather be heading back to Viewhill for a smoke and something cool to drink, but she seems pretty adamant, so I agree and follow her towards the square and the thickening crowd.

If memory serves, the suits have recently gathered in Brighton or Blackpool or somesuch similar pensioners' Mecca for their annual bleat about how great things are, and how much greater is to come, and how grateful and humble we should all be, and promising earnestly to string up all nerrdowells by their jarlers for stuff like littering and swearing and such, all that type of banter. So whatever the suits say about the rates hikes has caused much stink and unhappiness and these demos have been expanding in size and intensifying in bitterness, and many warnings are coming from like on-high about how the civil disobedience is not tolerable and will be met with this and that and whatever other, and it all sounds a bit teachery and harsh, but the punters continue to gather all the same.

Of late I've seen some of these demos from my elevated position in Viewhill, usually on Friday mornings for some reason, and on these mornings, invariably rainy and glum, those with an interest in such dryness wave banners and walk towards the town and gather with others, and start to sing, and head for the George for a bit of a shout at the councillors before heading to the boozers and the buses and letting it lie for another week. This has been going on for maybe three or four months. But the demonstrators are never allowed to actually enter the George itself, the rozzloiders always cordoning off the whole square so that the shouters and flag-wavers are forced to move in a great big circle, which is really a square, and they're maybe allowed to do that three or four times, shouting all the while, before the cops start to shepherd them back to the main drags and they all disperse, leaving a few of the angriest to point their fingers at the rozzos or else throw eggs and empty juice cans at the council chambers, where there is no-one actually working on account of general fear.

Joanne tells me that this demo today has been organised and applied for through the very highest of official channels, and is being backed by big unions and some heavy business guys and so on, and that the shouters and flag-wavers are to be allowed to have a proper rally in the George, this all being regarded as something of a breakthrough, and a sign of possible back-down by the council, who might now arrange for an amnesty on the rates hikes which will cause much happiness on account of many slates being wiped clean.

So it's on this humid late summer afternoon that they've all come from near and far, all these disgruntled rates-affected punters, singing and shouting and threatening to do all sorts to Peetie McLimpson, this being the small and aged character with the upside-down face who happens to be the current Provost and is the target of much derision and hate. So me and Joanne are joining in all this merriment and howling and general rowdiness, hurling verbals at the rozzoids and anyone else who'll listen as the crowd kind of herds and swamps into the square.

The sun comes out, and it starts getting really hot. There's no stage as such, but a big lorry has been decked out with a microphone and sound system and banners saying this and that, and a good few bodies up there are milling about with wires, chatting and smiling and waving to their pals in the swelling crowd, and a tape of the new Fairly Road album comes on so that's quite popular and gets a few folk singing along.

The crowd's as big as any I've ever seen in the square, and that includes the New Year bashes they used to have, and even at those you only ever got in with a ticket. And the atmosphere's a bit like that actually. Quite happy and cheery, and there's a few cans of lager going about and I get a waft of hash here and there, so I'm pretty glad we came after all, and me and Joanne smile at each other and move forward nearer the stage, 'cos you never know if some celebrity might turn up and it'll be good to get a right good close up if they do.

The rozzlings are out in number as well, and they're in like a huge circle with arms going off the four main drags into the Square, and along these four arms are parked their Kalibros and the meat-wagons, all nice and military-style, and even a few bike-bound rozz dotted here and there, and even looking at the rozzer's transport hardware sort of adds to the carnivally feel 'cos they're painted so bright, with their orangey strips and pink bars along the back, they're like ice-cream vans, and surely there would be a roaring trade for them today if they were.

And Joanne's dead excited, all cheered up like I haven't seen her for weeks, and she pulls me along and we slide our way through the bodies and ever nearer the stage bus. It's kind of weird being in a crowd like this during the day, it's almost like you should be in a club in the wee small hours, all sweaty and a buzz in the air, but needing the darkness 'cos you're doing something wrong, or at least, if you want to feel you're having a good time then you should be, but this is daylight, and we're not doing anything wrong, so why it should be a buzz is kind of weird, but a buzz it most definitely is.

The tape gets switched off but bands of folk here and there start up their own stuff, and they're all trying to join up and sing together but it's not really working but they're having a laugh trying, and someone in another part of the square starts another song or maybe the same song at a different time, so that the words and the melodies all sort or merge and die and start up again and end up getting like swept about the square along with the flying rats, these being what we call pigeons.

So this guy with an ultra-bright white shirt starts running about on the stage hauling wires and tapping mikes and all that, then these others get up on the lorry. Joanne passes me a smoke but we don't have a light so I ask this wee guy in front of me, who's like a hundred and fifty or something, five-one at most and skinny-malinky and pure sweating and he takes out a lighter, all shaking hands and grunts and wheezing and all sorts. He's got these big red blotches all over his face, but not like birthmark scars, so maybe he's got cancer or somesuch and Joanne offers him a smoke as well which is maybe a bit dodgy if it is cancer that's all over him, but he takes one and emits many more grunts and wheezes by way of thanks, then lights us all up and turns away.

Maybe it's about ten minutes later, but not much more, and it starts getting really squashed, and it's ending up that I've got my face practically in the old guy's thin white hair, and I can hear him breathing, fast and shallow like he's got asthma or something, and I'm almost getting the boak what with being able to smell his hair and his papery old skin and thinking that those reddy blotches might be able to sort of jump right off him and onto me and that'll be me fucked with cancer.

There's a couple of girls behind me and they're getting really squashed as well, and it must be pretty bad 'cos one of them starts panicking and giving it gush and sob and I-want-to-go-home and all that to the other lassie, maybe her big sister, but it's getting more and more packed all the time behind us and the two girls eventually sort of slip in between me and Joanne, then the old guy, and try to snake their way further to the front, maybe hoping to get out that way. I don't really mind crowds and that but this is getting dodgy, and I can tell that Joanne's not enjoying it much either.

Joanne pulls my arm again, and I can hardly turn, but when I do I see her on tippy-toes giving it big wave and shouting how-you-doing to someone I can't see.

~ That's Bobby down there. Come on, says Joanne, and I, of course, go follow her like some sad puppy, as is my usual form these days.

So it's total murder getting through to the guy, but when we eventually do it turns out that he's got a bit of a perch on one of the plinths holding the big black glossy statue of some long-dead horsebacked city-father type.

Joanne's had a bit of a sweat for young Robert Harris, but she's been quite cool on the subject for a while and I haven't heard his name mentioned for some weeks. He's a nice enough wee guy, quite thin and wasted like he maybe has some mild needle problem, but his gear is cool and he has a nice smile. He always looks at me and Joanne a bit funny, as if he thinks perhaps we're an item. Or maybe it's because I don't smile too readily and he thinks I don't like him, but whatever, he's all big grins and can't be nicer.

~ Come on up! he shouts, and he bends right down and grabs Joanne's hand.

By the time she gets squeezed up there with the rest of them, all balancing on this like very thin ledge, there's no space at all for me, especially with me being slightly broader of beam than the slender Joanne, but sundry youths perched alongside her and Bobby do a very considerate shuffle to create a further gap, and I am duly hauled up. And even on this slightly elevated position the difference in the view is amazing, and we're even nearer the stage than before, maybe thirty feet or so away from it.

Atop the Council Halls there's a team of camera-folk, all shoulder-strapped vidders and tripods and such, scanning the George. Bobby points out others on top of the higher office buildings. A helicopter passes over, quite high right enough, doing a big arc way above, and that's maybe a radio 'copter doing the normal weather and traffic bumph, but then, a minute later, another 'copter comes in, lower and slower and this is certainly a rozz-copter, with bright stripes and numbers and letters, and that gets the biggest cheer of the day so far, all squinting upwards and roaring at it to fuck off and giving it the fingers, but it takes its time arching over the George before dipping out of sight, the noise staying a lot longer. And the mike is tapped along to the beat of the copter, which does eventually fade, and the guy with the big bright white shirt cracks a couple of limp jokes and introduces some suit or other.

I don't know the speakers, but Joanne, who's on the other side of Bobby, shouts over to tell me who's who, and Bobby, also being interested in such things, tells me a bit of background. So-and-so isn't a bad egg, but such-and-such is a brown-nosing two-faced fuck who's a cheek showing her face and this other one is trapped in the past, and it's all a bit dry for my liking but the last lassie is good, some housewifie from up our way, and she gets tore right in, suggesting that we might like to make a bit more space for ourselves by going into the Council Halls and making ourselves a cup of tea seeing as how it's our hall and our tea and if we're not going to be asked then we can be forgiven a one-off lapse in manners etc. etc. and that gets the crowd going good style. At first it's like a joke, and I don't know if maybe she's had a wee bead in her or perhaps she's one of those wifies who gets hammered into the tranquis as soon as she gets out of the sack, but she starts getting really sort of carried away and saying that we really should do it, that it's our cally and our city and if the bastard councillors won't turn up to do their job then why don't we just team in there and do it ourselves, her claim being that at least we would do it right.

So there's a few bodies down the front who do start

actually making their way over towards the front of the Halls, but the rozzlings are thick in force and stay well-put, reinforcements strolling in cool-style from the side drags. The rozz-copter suddenly reappears, much higher than before, and starts making a circle, in view all the while.

So this woman's really set the cat among the proverbials, and this suit has appeared and grabbed the mike off her and she's giving it laldy, trying to get it back, it's like something out of a bar brawl, and you can only hear snatches of what she's saying and he's saying, and it's almost all abuse, and the drumming of the 'copter above makes it impossible, so then the other bodies are getting into it, and a few punters are trying to get onto the stage from the crowd.

The boos start up close and loud, and this heid-bummer rozz with mega-glistening bunnet and fluorescent stripes suddenly strides right up onstage, two underlings in tow, grabs the mike and passes it to one of his boys. It's switched off. The heid-rozzer gets the woman and starts reading her the works, but she's still game for him, maybe she's gone into like hysteria or something, and even with the racket from the 'copter and the crowd you can hear her screaming fuck you, fuck off and all that, and every time she does the crowd gives it yoo-ha, so this burly underling rozzer makes a bid for her, gets her in like an arm-clamp and the other one helps and they all just march right off, dragging her in a fairly brutal manner which causes mighty upset, the cheers becoming very dark and angry and merging into a huge and rather scary thundery-type roar.

Someone close behind us, maybe on the next plinth, lobs a bottle. A glass bru bottle. It misses the rozzers, who by this time are dragging the woman off the back of the stage, but is almost immediately joined by a hail of other missiles, mostly empty cans. From where we are I can see the heid-rozzer talking into his jacket. The bottles are starting to fall atop the rozzers stationed afront the Council Halls, and the bunched yellow coats get closer together, bowing their skulls and turning their black round hats towards the crowd by way of paltry defence. But the missiles start to connect, and the roar of the punters is now a nasty thing altogether, filled with screams and the sound of genuine panic. Those below us start shoving forwards, but it's hard to tell if they want to, or are just being forced to by those behind, and looking at them it's impossible to say if they want to either. It's like the crowd is getting sucked towards the Halls, and can't stop, even if it tried to, and it's like within a few seconds it's turned into one of those mad surges you see on old football games, and thank fuck we were where we were and not down there.

But right then Joanne starts trying to get down. Bobby jumps, holds his hands up for her. She jumps, then they both help me, and right away I make for the nearest drag.

~ Where are you going? Joanne shouts to me, wide-eyed and flushed, and I'm amazed that she is actually enjoying this, which by her expression she surely is.

~ Where the fuck do you think? I shout back, home!

But I'm going nowhere fast 'cos the surge comes again and it's a definite suicide shot to try and get across it to the side-drag, so I turn back and get myself in firm against the base of the plinth. The bodies pour past, like stones in a river, bouncing off each other, getting

squashed for a few seconds against someone or something, then getting pushed around it or them and
flowing on. I've got a good grip on the stone base of the
statue. Joanne and Bobby have gone altogether now,
and even though I know they can't be that far away
there's no chance of seeing them unless I get back up on
that plinth.

I stay put for a minute, hoping a gap might appear so
I can make a bid for Glassford, but the bodies slow and
start to get madly compact. Someone nearby must've
fallen cos there's a really blood-curdling scream that
you can't even tell if it's a man or woman, and it's so
muffled and horrific, then suddenly stops and starts so
you can tell that someone's being trampled. And there's
folk screaming to stop, and trying to give directions,
and then there's another one down and howling and
fights are happening and people are pulling at each
other, holding their kids up in the air, climbing onto
each other's shoulders. The screams spread, and even
the sound of the 'copter seems to fade even though it's
right overhead, and there's no shouting any more, no
roaring, no cans and bottles landing, no cheering, just
screaming from the entrance to the Halls where the
crowd has become a big solid unmoving lump.

The rozz-copter suddenly veers up and back and
away, but another comes in low to take its place, and
it's unmarked, maybe a news crew or suchlike, and at
the same time you can see the roofs of a couple of the
meat wagons pushing into the square, coming off
the drag to the left of the Halls, and also I can see the
assembled banners of all the folk who've not been let
in, and they're still coming forward. Maybe these other
punters have taken the general rumble and screaming

to be a sign of action and they want in on it, and it's like the same thing is happening at the other three drags into George, so that everyone is trying to get in, but looks like no-one is interested in getting out, though by the screams it's clear that this is not so. I know I want out and offsky but many others are not even in as fortunate as situation as me, and I'm staying well put.

I get myself up on the lowest of the plinth's ledges, and even this is just a couple of feet off the deck but now I can see. No sign of Joanne and Bobby. The vans open and the riot rozz start jumping out, all black shininess and thick plastic shields, and the Halls' massive black double-doors open right at the same time and a solid team of similarly clad riot rozz come belting out, giving it deep grumbly roar, banging their thick sticks on the shields and behaving in a tribal and beastly fashion which brings more shouts of fear in angry reply. The crowd tries to surge inside the Halls, but they only get a few feet before the sticks are extended and the shields are coming down on heads like dustbin lids and folk start going down and it's soon like an invisible wall at the stairs into the Halls, and those who cannot get away tumble into the pile and are being severely seen-to if they get beyond it. I think I catch a glimpse of Joanne quite near the Halls' entrance, but the brief flash of blonde is swallowed and I soon lose the place what with the seasick-inducing movements of the crowd.

By now the noise is totally unreal, like it just keeps getting louder and can't be turned down at all, and then, I josh not, this team of horsebacked rozz appears from the goods entrance to the train station, which is like a normally quiet and rather decrepit looking ramp which slopes into the building housing the north-bound rail traffic, and the horses are stiff-eared and rearing and giving it loud and frightening horse noises as their riders urge them into the crowd, and just at this time a siren goes off somewhere and I'm sure my ears will burst, like someone is stabbing knitting needles right inside them, so I turn, pure panicking now, mercury aslop, and start clawing my way up the plinth, trying to get back to where we were earlier.

Someone tries to pull me down as I start hauling up to the highest ledge, but there's no way I'm staying down there, and it's this older guy who's grabbed me and he's screaming as well, but I just let one arm go, turn half-way and elbow him a cracker right in the face and he sort of howls and drops onto the bodies below. Someone else grabs at my leg as I'm almost up, but I kick and kick and connect with something softish, get free, and right away I look to see if there's any way of getting further up, there being nothing further to mount bar the statue itself. I manage to get a hold of the horse's tail, and I'm surprised that it's actually quite hot to touch, what with the black metal absorbing the bright sun, but it's a good shape to get a hold of, and with a mighty haul, then another, I get on the back of the thing, shimmy along then grab the city-father's coat-tails, then another serious haul and I'm up and astride the shoulders of this long-dead bastard and I sit with arms wrapped about his head, legs fastened about his chest, and I can see it all, hear it all, and closing my eyes doesn't help, and it's like hell is happening right there below me.

Maybe it's about an hour before I get back down. I wait until I'm sure I can make a clear run to the Glassford. By now the ambulances have managed to get through and the corpses are being loaded into the meat wagons. Bodies everywhere, mostly in a long heap covering the half-dozen steps up to the Halls' entrance, but dozens of others scattered throughout the square like so much rubbish among all the cans and bags and empty sweet-pokes and fast food boxes, and dozens of green-clad paramedic types go round the bodies as fast as they can, checking who's alive and signalling when they find someone who is. The dead are loaded into the vans pronto, and there's a few camera-snappers moving about. And the helicopter's still buzzing over every few minutes.

The van nearest me, with doors open, must have at least ten, twelve bodies piled inside, and at the bottom of the pile is the old guy, and I can't see his face but I can make out the large strawberry blotches, not as red as they were before, on his white-grey scalp.

One hundred and twenty three are killed that day in the George, and another thirty or so die afterwards, there being almost a thousand casualties. Sixty-something arrests, but the so-called Lord MacDonald Inquiry still hasn't even called any witnesses.

Joanne and Bobby had ended up inside the Hall, and were arrested along with another three hundred or so who piled through the riot boys by sheer force of number and thus avoided being trampled and suffo-cated by friends and family and co-demonstrators.

She was pretty pleased with herself I think, but maybe because she'd impressed Bobby rather than taken part in the battle. They became a sort of item in the days and weeks after the George, and they would come into the pool Hall together from time to time, arm in arm and generally quite gloopy to see. But at least she was happy, and it showed.

I know I didn't make a very great effort to disguise my dislike of Bobby. So, she had a boyfriend. That was no big deal. But what happened was that she started going over to his place all the time and I never got to see her. Even when I'd call and I knew she was home, there was nights she wouldn't even say hello, too busy with her Bobby. So I started having a dig at him now and then and telling her I thought he was dodgy for this or that or whatever reason, and this just made her mad and defensive. I should have kept my gob shut, for the more suspicions I voiced, which were borderline or just plain daft, I was coming out with them and thinking them for so long and so hard that I started to wonder if I was irrational about it all or there really was reason to dislike the guy.

But it was more than a simple jealousy I think. There was something about him that set me on edge. She brought him up to mine a couple of times, perhaps in the hope that I would want to knock about on the bag or whatever as usual, but I stayed quiet and drank tea on both occasions and let them watch videos, but as they were leaving the second time I took Joanne aside and told her straight out that I didn't like him and didn't trust him and I didn't want him inside my pad again and she went very white and mad and kind of stormed off.

The nightmares started getting worse about then as well. The screams in the George that day seemed to be sort of locked into my head, and if I fell asleep or maybe was daydreaming, they'd start popping up, a lassie nearby, a young guy shouting for his pal, and boots and shoes and heels on flesh and more screams until the feet become so thick and heavy that there's no movement except down, and everything on the deck cracks and spreads and oozes as more comes down, and Joanne's in there somewhere. Her and Bobby. Just that glimpse of blond and she was gone, and surely down under the thousands of heavy boots getting the air and the life crushed out of her. Then I wake up holding onto the pillow like I was holding onto that city-father's neck, and I pinch myself and say that Joanne isn't dead. It's just that she doesn't want to be my friend any more.

But now in the Hall, with pool balls clacking and the Flash starting to nibble at my brain, I pinch myself again and this time she is dead. And even if she did want to be friends again, it's too late.

CHAPTER THREE

~ You're up next, says Gerry, but I'm still sort of dazed and remembering the Battle of the George hasn't helped matters.

Gerry proffers the cue but I decline. She shrugs and beckons Danny with a head-jerk, then squeezes past where I'm sitting with back to the low-slung window. There's a draught hitting the back of my head but I don't care. I'm not in the mood for work at all, and still haven't decided who we should be trying to visit this evening.

It's definitely getting harder. After the Battle, things got so heavy that mostly everyone just gave their rate-books to the bin and the winds and the dogs, and this squad of seriously heavy suits got sent up from the capital to see if they couldn't muck about with the accounts and come up with something before the whole place became like a total war zone.

So it all comes to a head, this is maybe three or four

months after the George, and there's this special broadcast by your main man live on the box and the radio at the same time, and all the papers are full of it, and he lays out what's going to happen in a very smiley and comfortable manner which is familiar to all as the mode he uses when up to something nasty. The conclusion runs pretty much like this: the council has shown that it can't collect the dosh, and there's no way the government's going to do it on top of all the other collecting they already do, so from now on there's going to be what they've called Operation Community Responsibility, and this is a new and somewhat controversial scheme whereby individuals will be matched according to where they live and how much they earn, whether or not they have credit ratings etc, and they will have to collect the rates money from each other. If you don't participate, it's the jail, pure and simple.

Right away folk are kidding and joshing about it, treating it all like some huge joke, a big wind-up. It just doesn't seem possible. But sure enough, a few weeks later, everyone starts getting these forms in the door, and there's ads on telly to explain it all, and no-one's talking about anything else. My form comes through along with a wee pink payment book, and the name printed on the front is Imrie, Hugh.

Now, Hugh is the same age as me, left school the same time, and has long been a signer like the rest of us. Everyone calls him Shuggs and this Shuggs fancies himself as something of a ticket. He's always run with a crowd from the Spring called The Wee Burn, but he's been trying to make a name for himself in Viewhill so he can get to be leader for a change, and what with him filling out pretty spectacularly since he left the school, and with his predilection for occasional outbursts of extreme violence, he is doing not a bad job of it either. His Cherries, as they've now become pretty well known, have got a bit of rep now for knocking cars, general housebreaking and gratuitous villainry, but nothing too extreme yet anyway as regards physical damage to the person bar beatings and sporadic knifings.

So this payment book comes in, and I'm supposed to be collecting his rates dosh? No chance. Okay, his payment is barely four or five bucks per week with him being an official signer and all, but that's hardly the point. Presumably, and this is if we've understood the scheme right, this Shuggs would've been sent a payment book with my name on it, and I know for sure that if he turns up on my doorstep demanding cally then he'll be heading back to the Cherry basket with very swollen jarlers and a sore face to boot.

So I get Joanne and Danny together and we have a right good old gab about it all. With Joanne being over on the edge of the Spring, she's been landed with some name she's not too sure about, but reckons to be a girl from the General School who she knows by sight but isn't friendly with. Danny's match is another of the Cherries who she actually quite fancies so she's fairly smiley and goofy about it all, and looks at the wee pink payment book like it's some kind of Valentine's card.

Joanne has the paper with her this night when she comes up to see me, and Danny's stayed for her tea so we're all sat in the room huddled about the radiator, it being a February eve and cold enough to make you greet.

Danny's been coming up a bit more of late, and that's probably 'cos I sought her out and made contact and have been encouraging her. Danny's actually my sort of foster-cousin I suppose you'd say 'cos her Mum is my Mum's foster sister. Mum and Helen have got like twenty years between them and they never really saw that much of each other anyway what with Gran dying so young. Helen was working so she couldn't look after Mum. They drifted apart then. But come Christmas Mum always got a card from Helen, and she'd then send one back, but always have to rake about for the address. I only met Danny about three or four times when we were wee, and it was usually at some funeral or wedding or suchlike, and I don't remember Mum talking much to Helen even then. Me and Danny would sort of hang about with each other and end up scrapping more often than not, but we seemed to get on okay.

So when Joanne starts not coming up at all rather than not have dearest Bobby on her arm, I call Danny one Saturday and we go for a drink and talk about what's happening and it's all pretty cool. She's trying to get a job, but she says she wants to work for herself, be a businesswoman. She's all full of ideas about shops and mail-order stuff and it's all a bit ambitious, I think, but she's surely keen enough. Pains me to say it, but Danny is not the sort of girl who would cut a dash in a pin-stripe business suit, black ribbon tightly holding down the combed-back hair. No, indeed, no. Danny is almost six feet tall, and has the kind of body many eighteen year old men would gladly swap for. And it would be easy to get the impression that this thickness of body is matched intellectually as dearest Danny has trouble with basic sums and spelling, and trying to read a newspaper is apt to cause her much angst and distress.

So Danny has as much chance of starting up her own business as I do, and I rate those chances at near or about zero given that I have no desire at all to work for myself or for anyone else, and wish solely to be left alone to do what I do, that is, training and films and eating and sleeping.

We've got a three-litre pot of Lemon Splinter and enough for a few joints, but it's so cold that we prefer to stay still sitting on the floor under the quilts wrapped about our shoulders. Danny has been going on about getting a job and she's had this heavy bumph through saying that if she doesn't get one of her own accord she'll be given a Community self-help job, and these always involve grottiness such as clearing the banks of rivers or maybe searching hedges for needles, so Danny is quite hyper about getting something half-decent, and soon.

Joanne says hers in the library is going alright, and she gets to use the computer they've got in the records office, and it's like this newest of super-chic cutting-edge consoles with the very latest facilities and full web access and all that, so she's chuffed and very rabbitty about it all. I'm honestly quite happy for her but I don't ask her that much about it cos I don't really understand what it is she does. She says it's to do with data retrieval and security, and she actually gets to devise programmes and such, and this seems to be a real major thing. Plus, she says, the money's good and she ends up paying nearly all the time if she's out with Bobby, and it gets on her wick now and then but he's worth it.

So eventually she kind of quiets and slows and maybe realises that she's gabbing too much in a like boastful and bragging manner which does not at all suit her, and it's maybe a guilt thing, but she points out this ad under the Sits Vac.

She stays quiet as I read this thing carefully. It's asking for people to become Liaison Officers for the Commissioner's Office, this being the collective name for the heavy suits who've made up the love-thy-neighbour rates scheme. Although this ad doesn't give any details of payment, it says something about exceptional remuneration, which I take to mean that it's pretty good.

At first I think Joanne's showing me this 'cos she reckons it's a decent job, so I make like I'm enthusiastic and say I'll call it. Well that sets her off then, and she starts on about how it's a lot of shite, and she's pointing it out 'cos it's an example of what not to get into, how it's really dodgy and maybe even illegal.

Danny gets me to read the ad out to her, and she kind of nods and gets bright-eyed and you can tell right away she's interested, and this sets Joanne off again, on about how folk shouldn't do the bastards' work for them and it'll just cause further problems down the line if we do.

But by this time it's backfired, well-meaning as perhaps it was. She's getting right high and mighty, and easy for her to do when she's already in such a pretty plum position, so I decide to set my face against her and say I'm going to find out about it. Danny also voices her curiosity, and I call the 24-hour number and this computer voice asks questions and tells me that my information is being sent directly so we get back to the

Lemon Splinter and roll a number and gas about things in general, forgetting about this scheme and related trivia, saying we'll wait for the bumph to come to find out the score.

The bumph comes in the second post the very next day, and the score is very simple indeed. The Commissioner's boys know fine well that going door-to-door is no longer a viable option for their staff, there being such a wild hatred of them now that serious assault is a certainty should they show face, even in areas perhaps previously regarded as 'respectable'. As Liaison Officers we'll be expected to collect on behalf of those in our neighbourhood who cannot or will not undertake the task i.e. the vast majority, scared to venture out of their doors to go to the pee-oh or The Depot let alone marching up to a neighbour's door with open palm and demand for cally. The Officers get to keep a straight fifteen per cent of all monies collected and personal liability will be guaranteed at a fixed annual cash sum for the duration of the scheme, which is expected to be at least three years and may be permanent, and the fixed bi-annual cash performance bonus is also guaranteed to be at least five times the current signers allowance, and will be tax-free. All things considered, it looks an attractive package right enough, and if I've got the sums right in the wee booklet they enclose to work out the arithmetic of it all, it seems that we could, if working in a team of three or four, reasonably expect to clear somewhere between four and five tons a week – each.

It's a strange thing to ponder having money. It starts me imagining about what I would do. Dream-chasing is what Joanne always calls it, when you get worked up thinking about what you don't have and what you could have. She says it's like hypnotising yourself into believing something that you don't really believe at all. She says she doesn't want money, and she doesn't need it, and that's great coming from someone who's in a family where they've never been what you would call spit-poor, and she's in a job already and she's just eighteen.

We've never really argued about anything, but the money thing starts to eat into me, and I find myself asking why I shouldn't have some. If it involves getting nasty with folk then that's not a problem. I want to fight and I will fight, so I'd be as well getting paid for it. That's not to say that I would do friends or family. Of course I wouldn't. But I would surely do anyone who did any of them. So as long as I know who we're getting heavy with, there shouldn't be a conflict of interests. I fill in the forms and get copies of my school grade papers and birth certificate and such and help Danny with her form and we send them off at the same time.

So when the wee slip comes through saying that I've been accepted for the training course and should prepare to be away from home for two weeks I'm pretty much as cock-a-hoop as is possible for me to be. Danny gets her wee slip in the next day, and we go out that night to The Hall and get well and truly wrecked, gabbering on great style about how loaded we'll be and what sort of gear we'll get, and Danny gets so excited and generally drunk with like optimism and happiness that she heads off to one of the pool tables and actually asks this guy out, this Pinkston nephew she's fancied for ages, and the guy's mortified and tells her to fuck off but she stays calm and charming and his mates are giving him some stick over it and then she like grabs him like an old black and white of Clark Gable with some wench and gets him backwards and she's holding him up and she gets wired right into him and his pals roaring and cheering all the while. I sit and laugh like I haven't for ages, and all the time I'm tying to work out how I can get Joanne into this as well 'cos I know it won't be the adventure it should be unless she's on board, and more to the point, I fear I'm losing her friendship for good.

~ I'm not doing it. It stinks, says Joanne, and you're a fuck-up if you do.

I've never ever lost my temper with Joanne, but I'm very close to it this day.

~ It was you pointed out the fucking thing, I say, and anyway, you're the one who's always moaning on and ever about cally and getting a nine-to-fiver. Well, this isn't as dry as you might have me down for, but tell me what shop'll give me that type of dosh for dressing dummies?

She stays sort of silent and morose, frowning in the spring sun as we sit outside Magenta, this likely being one of very few chances to absorb some natural light before the weather takes another bastard turn and the showers of April arrive.

The two weeks at the course it rained solid, and when it didn't we were in the classrooms getting topped up with statistics and basic computer skills and all manner of similar bumphology, and a mighty struggle it all was for Danny, who was most reliant on yours truly for basic pointers. The outside stuff was better, when they tested our fitness and demonstrated some self-defence stuff, and that was scooshy for me and Danny alike, but fun nonetheless and a chance to show some of the other trainees what we could do by way of kicks and punches and sundry other techniques when the official self-defence stuff was over.

And a lot of these other trainees have sound ideas about how they're going to operate, and a lot of them are older guys who've done a bit of army stuff and maybe got chucked out or didn't even get in for various crime and drug-related naughtiness, and what with some of these characters having experience as debt collectors we hear many stories, some exaggerated no doubt, of near misses and close shaves involving packs of dogs and ambushes and blade-wielding razzos and other such scarifying stuff. Not that we are to be called, or refer to ourselves as debt-collectors – we are always to use the name Liaison Officer, as this name is supposed to convey the co-operative and facilitating nature of our task.

Also, with it being a fortnight on this very like varied and wholesome menu every day, but not too much of it, me and Danny both come back off the train from Inverness looking like we've just been in some sort of health camp, and it's only the last few days now that the glow has gone from my cheeks and I'm back to being like dough-grey.

We arranged to meet here on the edge of the swing-park, but Danny's late as usual, and when I do spot her making her way up from the bus stop I'm surprised and not a little annoyed to see that she's got another lassie with her. I told her we were supposed to be talking business, so the presence of this interloper annoys me.

Joanne stays silent as they approach, as do I, and it is a thick and murky silence indeed.

~ Girls, this is Kelly, says Danny, she's up for it.

Danny's tone suggests that she's maybe expecting a medal or somesuch in return for this unwelcome development, instead of which she gets two dirty looks and a share of the murky silence.

~ Well, looks like someone isn't up for it, say I, and that's the one who got everyone wound up about it in the first place.

It maybe sounds a lot mowlier than I intended, but Joanne gets up pronto.

~ I'm not doing it, and that's that, she says. Different if it was like a desk-job, all above board and that, but this is just legalised gangery, and if you do it you'll end up no better than any of those sad krewes up Mayhill and everywhere else. I'm happy in the library, and whatever you think of it doesn't much bother me one way or other. I'm not stopping you doing it, but you can't make me. And don't dare say it was my idea that you should. See you about.

And with that she turns away and walks kind of slow and aimless down towards the footbridge which will take her over the motorway and down to the back end of the Spring. I watch her stop on the footbridge, and she leans over, watching the traffic streaming below.

~ Well, that's that then, I say, and turn my attention to Kelly.

And this Kelly is really a lovely girl, but so thin and small, she doesn't look at all up for what is likely to be a tough job.

~ Well, you said we need another body, says Danny now.

I nod, but as far as I'm concerned we still need two. This lass is a balsa-wood barbie.

~ I know someone, says the small creature called Kelly, and a nice voice it is, a bit girly, but strong and cheerful, like she hasn't noticed the expression of incredulity I've been wearing since her approach.

~ Who's that then? I ask.

~ Gerry North, she replies as I stand up and face her. The name suddenly registers, and I burst out laughing.

~ Are you taking the piss or what? I say, still smiling, but Kelly frowns, as if genuinely hurt that I don't believe her.

~ You never told me you know her, says Danny.

~ You never asked, Kelly replies, and I like her style now.

It's as if she's talking about a telly programme or a magazine or something similarly throwaway and light-weight. Gerry North's case had been all over the papers and box about three years previous – she murdered her own brother (stabbed him through the heart with a screwdriver) when she was only twelve and he was a much larger and genuinely nasty sixteen, but she got off after the prosecutor's office made an arse of the evidence and she'd been released to much hoo-haa and general alarm. That was all up Aberdeen way and she'd sort of disappeared off the map as far as the papers and that were concerned, and was technically a probation-hopper.

~ She would be ideal, I say.

~ And what about me? Kelly asks, and there's colour now to her face and I notice that she's staring at me really hard.

~ Alright, I say, let's give you a wee tester then.

Kelly steps back a pace, and there's a flash of anger in her eyes which is encouraging. She moves around to face me properly as I take a step nearer, and I notice that she's allowed her knees to bend slightly, always a sign of someone who knows a bit.

~ Don't take this personally, Kelly, say I, but I'm going to try and slap you. Not hard. I'll just try to slap your neck. I want you to try and stop me, then try and hit me back. Right?

She takes in a deep breath as she nods, then steps just a little closer, which also surprises me given that I've already warned her who'll be doing the first slapping. I stay with arms loose by my sides, staring her out. The sun is right behind her, and I squint just a little to keep the glare down. She shifts to my right, and with a clearer view of her face I can see her pupils tighten their grip on mine as I check my mercury and feint with a hip move to loosen up. Kelly shimmies back a step and brings her hands up, palms facing me.

For all the years of the karate and the kick boxing and sundry other sports of contact variety, I feel a tad shaky and trepidatious, as if about to be made a numpty of.

And I almost am. I raise my right hand fast and clean, but she parries it with her left and gives me a tremendous slap across the jaw which shocks and staggers me. I reach for her throat with my left but she's already snaked round to my side and before I can swivel she hammers a fist into my kidneys real sharpish. This wee fucker is not playing cutesy by any means. I'm quite badly winded by the punch, but with a rapid, and truth be told, accidental shuffle, I come close enough so that

I can grab her hair with my left, pull her close to my back, then hoist her right over me and bring her slamming down onto the pavement. Looking on it now, it's a rash move cos we're so close to the wall. I could easily break the runt's back, and I can hear Danny let out this sort of panicky scream as Kelly hits the deck.

But up she gets after two seconds or so, cleans the dirt off her white jeans, smoothes her blonde hair back into place and takes a seat on the wall as if she's just been skipping. She starts sniffing like mad and takes a big like lettuce of already well-used hankies from a pouch and blows into it. At first I think maybe she's greeting but then she looks up at me, bright-eyed and cheery again.

~ Well? she asks, and I hold her stare for a second.

~ Yeah, I say, trying not to grimace as the pain surges out like sunlight from my back. Yeah, you're in.

~ And what about Gerry? she says then, the end of her wee nose glistening with fresh snot in between blows.

I have to give myself a mental nip. Joanne has walked off, and within minutes, my team of little ladies is in place. It must be some sort of kismet-style fate thing. Gerry North?

~ Yeah, I say. Bring her along. My place. Tonight.

So it takes a wee while, what with getting a system organised, adapting our body clocks to the task of being out and about until the small hours, but it works. We use my place as the main base. With Mum working away I've the run of the flat. Danny uses Mum's room week-days, moves back to her Mum's at week-ends. Kelly and Gerry move into a vacant one-roomer two floors down from me. The CO's people come and install a smartish-looking data terminal for me to do the books and such, and we're given a healthy advance on wages to get uniforms. We've free choice clothing wise, and opt for combination of black and white leggings, tops and sweats, quilted short jackets, top of the range Pedro steel-toed boots and matching accessories, gloves, caps, earmuffs, the whole works. We get most of the gear on a one-day jaunt in Edinburgh, and it has to be said it's a bit of a buzz altogether, being able to shop in the very chicest of depots and not having to worry about the cally.

The door starts going at all hours – this one from the first floor, all sweaty and crimson what with just having rubbed up against Shuggs and his merry cherries, or else one of the other CO teams now operating, that one struck dumb with fear, bearing the tell-tale odour of involuntarily released bodily fluids. Sometimes, if the client has actually suffered physical damage we'll be straight out there and then to find those responsible, Shuggs more often than not, and he's usually to be found with his raggle-taggle collection of bum-fluffed Cherroids in their favoured Maxwell's Lounge by the river, and it'll be a few shouts at the door and they'll be out, swinging whatever is to hand and making light of our being the opposite sex or whatever.

Three times so far we've done that, but it's getting dodgy now, and other Maxwell clients have taken to accompanying Shuggs and his little boys, such is the sad response of the lad to a wee bit of confrontation. I suppose they must spend a pretty penny in there right enough, so it will pay Mr Maxwell to make sure Shuggs can frequent the place unmolested.

On the three occasions we did go down, we got away

with no more damage than is to be expected when you take on silly young boys, but they were limping back inside the club, no doubt to howls of derision from their peers, with ears torn and jarlers swollen and heads hung low and red. Of course, there comes a stop to it, and that's when we go down on behalf of old Mrs Stirling, who was seen that day by a couple of Shuggs's more ebullient underlings. No more than thirteen or fourteen, the pair of them, but they made a right mess of her as she emerged from the pee-oh with her pittance of a weekly allowance. She's on their list for maybe a couple of quid, but not content with that sum, they blag her entire wad, leaving her rooked and desperate, and kick her shins and knock her stick away and generally frighten her so fiercely that she shakes like a battery-operated toy and cannot speak when I open my door to her.

It is all quite distressing for me too, as Mrs Stirling is maybe one of the longest in the Magenta, and very kindly and smiley a soul she is too, ultra fond of children and prone to chatting and distributing toffee whenever she has it. Kelly makes some tea for her but she cannot even lift the cup without shaking it all over herself, and she sits quiet and sobbing and shaking all the more.

So we take her, bruised and grazed up and still shaking, to the safety of her one-roomed pigsty. Kelly calls the social team and they say they'll be out next morning to see her, but Mrs Stirling is purely sure she wants no rozz involved, and that's maybe as well.

Within half an hour we're making a bold approach to Maxwell's, suitably fired-up with a quick half-Flash at the Hall, and tooled accordingly, but we're not even

within shouting distance of the lounge when Shuggs
and troops emerge, veritably weighed down with
swords of Samurai style and a variety of other chibs.
There being but the four of us and twelve or more of
these young pretender Cherroids, we turn and beat a
retreat of hastiest sorts to Magenta, with Shuggs and
entourage scuttling behind very close and threatening-
like.

We get down to Magenta court entrance and I'm
screaming and gesticulating our predicament to Kieran
the Door, but he's neck-deep in the daily rags as usual,
no doubt bemoaning the performance of some horse or
other, and is very slow off the mark releasing the lock.

So that might well be us there and then. It's certainly
the best chance Shuggs has ever had. Gerry and Kelly
are standing their ground, with Danny between me and
the door, and there's just a split second when we might
be able to pull back together and get inside and then it's
just a matter of holding them back until the doors slide
shut and secure. But one of these younger Cherries
comes advancing, clearly full of something more than
happy juice, and he makes a mad lunge at Kelly with his
blade which is a short-handled fishing-type gutting
implement, and this inspires another couple of these
boys to make a bid for Gerry as the others stand
cheering them on, and with this perhaps being some
sort of laddish initiation-type thing, Shuggs and his
usual cronies are standing back when they would
normally be steaming in. Kieran the Door is out the
front doors by this time, roaring at us to get inside but
it's too late.

Gerry steps aside neat and throws the first of these
initiates over her shoulder as he runs straight into her,

and he obligingly rolls close enough to Danny for her to crack a heel down on his neck, setting him spinning like a car-struck cat, hands atop his crust like he fears imminent death by Danny-stomp. But Danny leaves him to spin and shriek and advances on the second of the youngsters and with a great swoop of her big arm she manages to grab his very tenderest of parts. Gerry already has him by the collar and is holding off the short sword-wielding hand, and this gives Danny the freedom to mangle his jarlers in one fist while chopping at his neck with other open palm.

Kelly is also managing to keep her assailant at bay with rather balletic swipes of her own little pen-flicker, and you can see the fear in the boy's eyes overcome at the prospect of the sure and severe embarrassment he will face if he flees, and as he is momentarily distracted by the great horrible screaming now coming from his colleague with the crushed nuts, Kelly sees the hesitation, moves forward quick and low and brings the blade clean across his abdomen, then ducks down further yet again and swings lower still, bringing the blade up in a straightforward punch that snaps him over double, and his little fish-filleter tinkles onto the pavement a second before he crumples atop it, silent and still.

Shuggs now steps forward, grabs the youth who Danny has released, and throws him back into the assembled Cherries. Gerry and Kelly stay tight together, Danny now beside them. Time for me to move to the front. Shuggs looks to have aged a good bit since I last saw him some months back and his eyes are very baggy and dark like he's in need of a serious kip.

~ You and me, Suzy, he says kind of shaky and all

filled up like I've just killed his dearest Granny or some-such loved one.

Those of his Cherroids who remain able-bodied have now bunched tight afront their wounded apprentices, and are undoubtedly waiting for the word. There are still too many for us should they choose to come ahead in team formation, and I know they must know that. But still Shuggs paces forward low and steady in apparent readiness for a one to one.

So my cutter is out and open and, with right arm extended, I'm within four feet of his blade, both steels glinting orange. He's like drawing something in the air with his, like it's a spell he wants to use rather than the weapon, then he shifts in fast and this is maybe the signal they awaited, for the patient Cherroids now pile upon us. Kelly gets in front of me and is waving and slashing like mad on my right, Gerry on my left and big Danny right out there in front, roaring her head off like she's maybe taking some sort of fit. The next seconds are long and full of movement, but there's too many of these bastards altogether, and I fear we're taking a terrible caning right now, and maybe it's our own fault, but I know my mercury is seriously sloshing around, and one minute I'm off my feet and the next I've got a hold of Shuggs about the waist and I've him raised off his feet and I'm like hammering my knee into his groin and stomach and at the same time he's clawing and battering at my back and one of his uglier buddies is taking pot shots at the side of my face. Danny screams again, and I stagger back with Shuggs still afront me and I make another mad swipe with my blade but it's a sort of desperation now 'cos he's getting dimmer and dimmer and the siren seems very far away.

As I slump to knees I hear Kelly yelling abuse at running footsteps, and I'm on my back on the grass and the cold night is rubbing my hands and face and the grass is warm and wet underneath. Gerry is over me, then Danny, then Kelly and Kieran the Door, and then I'm falling asleep and Gramps Pink is the last face I see as quiet nothingness wraps about me and when I next open my eyes I'm sweaty and startled and the smell of disinfectant is on my tongue and there is hospital white all about.

Gerry took a fair old whack on the skull from some sort of pathetic axe-type implement, this being the sort of sad tool favoured by younger Cherroids, and Danny had a broken nose and cracked collarbone. Kelly had little more than cuts and bruises, and seemed almost brassed-off that she hadn't received a proper injury as such.

Mine was the worst, I suppose, not that it pleases me much to have to admit it, but naughty Shuggs had indeed managed to get a good old dig at my back with his blade, and the coats told me it was just as well he'd connected with my spine in the angle that he had or else I could well have been deprived of the use of my lower limbs. And he opened up a fair old flap which resulted in the loss of much of my personal allocation of blood, requiring a multitude of stitches to close and the borrowing of many other people's blood. To make it all worse, I was then required to visit lechy old Doctor Fraser once a week for a month so he could check my right arm was working as it should, there having been suspicion of damage to some nerve or other.

So after many hours of gibbering and arguing and

even more hours of quiet pondering and vivid dreaming, it was pieced together with the input of all concerned, and it seems that if the Pinkstons hadn't come down when they did then it would surely have been the end of Suzy and her little ladies. That's when the friendship with Gramps really was cemented I suppose, and I had him to thank more than most, for it was indeed old Gramps who'd helped Kelly get Shuggs off me, and he'd stuck about and kept a kind of watch over proceedings as his sons and nephews and sundry family friends had a spot of exercise with the Cherries. Kieran the Door had, of course, alerted the rozzloiderlings, and the whole episode had even merited a couple of inches in the evening rag, mainly on account of Kelly's attacker having very nearly died in the central Hospy due to serious disruption of his innards and accompanying loss of personal blood allowance.

There was rozz-hassle, of course, what with the giving of statements and such, but no charges were brought. It went without saying that all said nothing when asked what they saw or knew, and in any case, it was just a run of the mill bunching of rival low-life having a territorial, and no-one really cared that much. In fact, truth be told, no-one cared at all.

CHAPTER FOUR

~ Are you playing or what? says Danny yet again, and sounding properly fed-up.

I double-grunt decline, pass her the dosh for the next round.

~ Make it pints this time, but sink them smartish. We'd best be heading soon, I reply.

~ So, where's it to be? asks Kelly, and she's already getting a bit edgy and jumpy the way she always does when the Flash starts to kick in, plus I see now that she's blagged a half-joint from someone.

~ What have I said to you about the smoking when we're working? I ask without even looking at her, still pretending to read my little numbers book.

She doesn't reply, just drops the chubby brown joint in the nearest ashtray and moves back to the table to set up the next game. I reach over, take up the stubby roach and draw the bones out of it before passing it to Gerry. This is hopeless. We're all in slow-motion, and no immediate prospect of things speeding up unless I get a grip.

Kelly, even as it is, is probably too far gone to work properly – she's hyper with the Flash but the smoke tends to dull and slow her, so if we're in a scrap and she ends up with her face hanging off she'll have no-one to blame but herself. Danny's performance earlier is still bugging me, and Gerry's near-gushiness over Joanne is unsettling. Overall, it's bad stuff. My little ladies are not on good form, nor am I.

I play but the one game of pool – a miserable loss against an admittedly sharpish Danny – then return to the corner and the dregs of the Flash, all concentrating now on the book, determined that the night will not be a total waste. All five names I end up underlining are overdue, and they all happen to be resident in the Cherry basket, so that's perhaps not total coincidence, but I know that the chances of encountering Shuggs and Co is still remote. But the listed are all young Cherries, all likely to be out and about what with it being their cheque arrival day, and it's just a matter of finding them and avoiding whatever renegade wanderers may have strayed in from the Spring or the Rucky.

So the ladies aren't too happy about having to leave the Hall and get back out into the freezingness of the late evening, but once we get a head of steam up, and are about halfway to Magenta, they liven up a bit and Kelly cracks a couple of jokes which go down well and even I allow myself a smile.

We're just past the playing fields and about to cross the unlit patch to the path when Danny, who's out in front, suddenly stops dead and holds a hand up to indicate we should do likewise. She has good eyesight does our Danny, a lot better than mine, and she's spotted something. I follow her raised forefinger, squinting to try and make out what she's pointing at. At first I can't see a thing, but then there's a movement, a good bit beyond the blocks, on the footbridge leading down to Cerulean East entrance. It's a squad right enough, and even with my poorer peeper performance I can make out about twenty five, maybe thirty bodies, loosely bunched in twos and threes and dallying about their progress.

~ That's not the Cherries anyroad, says Danny, and I see no reason to doubt her.

It's rare for the Cherries to venture any further East than the foot of the actual bridge, there being nothing beyond it bar the brewery-path, and even if they were using that route, they never would chance moving in a team of that size.

The mob stops in a darkened patch by the end of the bridge where the lights have failed. It's a patch we know well, where we occasionally take reluctant payers to persuade them of the error of their ways. Even Danny is having bother making out what's happening, so we hang back by the fence at the playing field and watch and wait.

It's not such a windy night, but now and then we get a very faint sound of muted laughter, and for some reason these soft wisps of laughter send a slight but certain chill through me which is most unusual as I am not given to attacks of panic or terror. Maybe it's just that you don't expect to hear any human sounds coming from the brewery-path at all by night, and when you do, it's always best to beetle off pronto. But it's something more. It's maybe because the laughter sounds controlled, not the usual drunken loutish roaring. But whatever it is, it makes me scared, just for a split second, and anything that scares me, even for a half second, also makes me very mad, and I swear that the hairs on my head and arms and even the tiny wee hairs on my legs and everywhere else, they all uncurl and point out the way when I get a shiver like that, and I feel right pointy and like cat-snarly now, all hackles up.

~ Anyone any ideas? I ask.

~ Maybe the Hills out for the night? ventures Gerry, but with no great conviction, and the suggestion receives the silence it deserves.

We all know there's no-one resident locally, or within walking distance, who would dare brave the brewery-path at night. By day it's a decent enough short-cut to the bus stops serving the East End, but early Winter darkness brings out the wannabes, the Powery Tiddlers, the Rebel Sons, Double-E Mini Crew, and a whole host of other small outfits who are to be avoided. Mostly in twos and threes, they will rob whatever drunks and needlers they come across, preferring to keep themselves well away from the main drags. They're usually very young, sometimes only eight or nine years old, and they are as dangerous as fuck.

This crowd loitering in the dark patch is not a crowd of teenagers. This is a serious squad. And their being in brewery-path land throws up two obvious explanations – they must be as heavy as heavy can be and fear no ambush, or else they may be strangers who have wandered in from other parts and are unaware of the danger. Either means that we may be now in a bit of a spot.

Kelly nudges me, and nods over to our dear home

Magenta, which lies maybe halfway between us and the shadowed crew. From the main entrance two rozzers emerge, fixing their bunnets and sauntering, chatting, to the parked Kalibro we haven't noticed. They get in and cruise quiet and slow down by Cerulean, taking them closer to where the shadowed team is motionless, only two or three of the figures visible by way of silhouette if you know where to look and stare really hard. No doubt they've seen the emergence of the rozz as well and are making like trees.

The long heavy car follows the road towards the footbridge, and although the brake lights briefly engage at the curve, it's too good to hope that these two little rozz will stop and enquire as to the team's well-being and activities, even if they do see them. Then the curve straightens and the bridge is overhead and the rozz are on the slip taking them onto the carriageway. And now the team advances once again, but tighter together than before and with a purposefulness of step which I find at once impressive and not a little dread-inspiring.

~ Time we got ourselves back home, ladies, I say, and it's Danny who pipes up yet again.

~ Home? I thought we had visits, she says.

I don't answer, but the speed of my walk must tell the ladies that my mind is made up. We're still in reasonably dense shade while we're by the fields, but within fifty feet or so of the path we'll be in view of this squad, and then, at best, we're equidistant from Magenta. The name keeps drumming through my head, with Gramps' big hand slapping on the table beating time – The Shaws, The Shaws.

No way. I still don't believe it. I haven't cracked a light to my little ladies, and I can imagine how mightily they'd scoff at the idea. And even now I'm still denying it, though alternative explanations are so few and far between as to be virtually non-existent. It crosses my mind that we might be best to turn back, head to the Hall and sit it out a couple of hours before returning, but that would not look good, especially as I don't yet know for sure who this mob are, and my standing would badly suffer were I to turn and flee from complete strangers.

We're still in what I think is the shaded zone, and there's time to turn and make a retreat back to the Hall when a shout goes up from one of the crowd, and the whole bastarding lot start running, almost at the Cherry basket. They've a slight hill between Cerulean and Magenta to negotiate, while we've a straight downhill run all the way. So I take off with my little ladies in close attendance, and I honestly don't know if we can make it. With our presence now well-noted and there being nowhere else within striking distance by way of safe destination, it's a no-choice all-out sprint.

The heavy-limbed Danny falls behind, so I drop back with her and let Kelly set a fine pace with Gerry close after, and they get to the doors just as the mob comes thundering over the wee hill by the Cerulean car park. Kieran is mercifully sharp tonight, and gets the doors open pronto. Danny is in a pretty bad way breathing-wise as I pull her through the last fifty yards or so, and the fastest of the strangers are bearing down with alarming speed.

Danny crumples through the doors with me virtually on her back as they slide shut in what looks like slow-motion and Kieran, hands shaking like nobody's business, throws on the manual switch and the security double-sliders whirr across.

Inside, with the blue foyer lights blinding us a tad, it's hard to see where the strangers are. I'm surprised they didn't get a bar or weapon through the door. They must surely have had time. But I can't see anything what with the reflections of the lights on the glass mixing with the reflections of me and Kieran and the puffing Danny, now crumpled on the deck heaving like a stranded water-beast, and also the reflections of Kelly and Gerry, close up and peering into the orangey darkness.

Then my eyes adjust a bit and I can make them out. They've stopped at the end of the grass, just on the rim of Magenta car park, and there must be forty of the fuckers. And well organised they must be too, for it seems to me that there is a definite formation about them, ordered and lined, like ready for inspection. This isn't a gang – it's a unit.

I know they can see me a lot better than I can see them, and have a quick glance about.

~ Get up, Danny, I order as I step back from the glass.

Kelly and Gerry are now beside me, and Danny lumbers up behind, still puffing like a not very magic dragon. I get a sudden flash of what we must look like to the crowd outside, and it's not exactly terrifying. Four young ladies, quite trendy and smart, but mightily out of puff and obviously a tad frightened, me bloated and flushed and anxious looking, and this thought makes me so mad that I want to tell Kieran to key in the double slider release code and let me out at the fuckers. Then I smile to myself at the sheer madness of such a thought, and what that perhaps says about my current state of mind.

Maybe you have to accept sometimes that things are out of your control. I don't like doing it, certainly, but moments come when you know you're just a spectator, and try as I might to stand tall and stop my chest heaving, and much as I want my little ladies to look the warriors that I know they most surely are, this is a moment when I know I just have to stand back and accept what's happening is not something that I have much say over.

Even with my less than perfect eyesight, I can see now that they are certainly not teenagers. They are dressed, for the most part, in dark one-piece dull boiler-suit type arrangements. Almost all are wearing close-fitting cloth caps. It's a pretty even mixture of guys and lassies as far as I can tell from basic physiques, but there's no telling for sure. A couple of them rest hands on knees, getting their puff back, but the bulk stare straight at us, arms folded, and I don't see much chit-chat among them and am wondering how long this staring game will last when one figure steps forward from the line, so cool and so steady, and this one has a belly full of mercury I'll bet.

She has to be the leader, and if she isn't, she should be. She stops after a few paces, and is maybe fifteen feet from the doors, just inside the pool of light cast by the overhead spots which are designed to help the vidder catch any villains plying their trade at Magenta's entrance.

She turns to her troops, and I can't hear anything being said but it's possible what with the double sliders being over that her voice is dulled, and my breathing is still heavy enough to have my heartbeat drumming in my cold ears. I get up to the glass and put my palms up against it and shield my eyes from the reception lamps and can see her a lot clearer now as she turns to face us again. She is a bit taller than me I guess, and older too, maybe mid-twenties. She's nice looking from a distance, in an old-style black and white film sort of way, all white and stark dark lips and heavy paint about the eyes.

She's smiling as she resumes sauntering towards us as cool as you like. Her eyes are wide, unblinking, like she's maybe on some speeder type pill, but you wouldn't guess it to look at her balance, like she's a replay of someone making down a catwalk. As she gets closer I can see that her gear isn't completely black. She's wearing a pair of militaresque grey-black breeks which I recognise from the camouflage pattern as being Original Rammer branded, and the jacket too is plain unpocketed dark-grey, a Webster Limited and mightily valuable too.

She pauses about six feet from the door. I suppose it's either reckless or else extremely brave of her, 'cos with her troops so far back now, we could quite easily get the sliders open and haul her inside if we were really sharp. But right now it doesn't seem the wisest of courses, especially as we don't know yet what might be concealed beneath that most desirable of jackets.

She stands, legs slightly apart, hands clasped afront her, staring as bold and clear as you like directly at me. Then she has a good gander at Danny, and I'm sure I detect a low cattish mowl emerging from my big-boned cousin. Another higher whine comes from Kelly behind, but I palm her into silence without turning, move forward myself, press my face against the glass to flatten my nose in authentic toddler-on-a-bus mode and smile hard at this stranger.

Despite her own smile, she has a saddish face, like one of those lassies who's always laden with weans and bags of provs from the Depot and worried about bills and rates and such, but it doesn't take much of a brainbox to work out that this is not your downcast and resigned type. There's a real beauty of a scar from the centre of her forehead right down to the chin like someone's cracked her with a largeish knife or sword. Her nose is sort of bumpy and shiny in places where you can see she must've had the old plastic padding job by way of repair and, while her make-up is neat enough, it's hard to imagine this woman has ever been what you would call conventionally pretty. Striking, yeah, but no teeny pin-up by a long stretch.

And to top it all, there's something about her that is familiar – not the face, that would be very hard to forget – something in her stance and movement and overall gait. I get the very distinct buzz that I have seen this stranger at some time before, perhaps at a distance, and perhaps some time ago, but I'm almost certain our paths have crossed before.

Then her smile disappears, and she's looking at the door frame, looking up at the vidder poised above which Kieran has undoubtedly now focussed in close, and then the smile returns as a theatrical, eyes-half-shut grimace. I hear Kieran's phone slamming down and his door opening, and somewhere away over in the Spring, a siren weakly starts. Not that that means much, and we all know it. The rozzloiders, probably the same two we saw just ten minutes ago, will let the thing blare and wail while they take the slow road back up via the Ruck, all sound and fury and going the roundabout way, their hope being that the disturbance will have been and gone and went for good by the time they arrive, just as the fuckers had been and gone and murdered my friend and vanished with many minutes to spare.

She sort of half-turns away, as if heading, then stops and turns back to face me, maybe ten feet away. It takes her three steps before she jumps, and it's the best kick I've ever seen. Her left foot is at least my head-height when it hits the door.

The doors for Magenta, like all others of standard double security block design, are triple plated, steel-ribbon reinforced and supposedly bulletproof. The crack is like a gun going off, and I jump along with the rest of my little ladies. She lands perfectly, that being something of a feat in itself given the rebound to be handled, then moves forward, brings her face right up to where the solitary crack has drawn a thin line down the outermost of the massive panes, and screams right onto the glass.

I find myself backing off, only a step or two, but backing off all the same. She's like something out of a vampire flick, all whiteness and mad eyeballs, mouth open wide, big long ugly tongue all fag-coated yellow-green, and broad strong palms press against the glass and it sort of creaks. She keeps her eyes on me all the time, not blinking, as she draws the tongue up the crack in the glass. It doesn't have the desired effect the first time so she does it again, and briefly screws her eyes shut as she forces her flesh against the razored edge, and this time the blood does come out, smeary greasy redness. A misty circular cloud of breath grows on the glass, then she uses her tongue to draw out two S shapes in the blood and saliva. But she does them backwards, as if for us to read.

She turns away then and paces back to her team as cool as before, through the centre of the line, then leads, walking them as far as the Cherry car-park before breaking into a light trot which becomes a jog as the Kalibro swoops under the footbridge, studiously ignores them, and makes for Magenta.

Kelly's already summoned the lift, but with the rozzloids' imminent arrival it's maybe safer to take the stairs. Kieran catches my eye as I pass his box, and he comes out as I stand with the fire escape stairs door ajar.

~ The cops was in few minutes back, Suze, he says, and I nod. Asked for you. I did my three monkeys. They weren't happy but didn't linger.

~ Cheers, Kieran, I say, and truly grateful-feeling I am, but the fear and weariness in my voice is something new to me, and even as we start the long hike up to home, my legs are heavy and unwilling and the siren slows and dies outside, and I let my little ladies go on ahead while I try to take on board the strange lassie and the SS in blood on the door, and for the first time in long enough my little pool of mercury has drained away to somewhere else and I feel well and truly scared.

There's a message from Mum onscreen when we get in, after saying goodnight to Kelly and Gerry, who look as done-in as I feel. Danny has, thankfully, fallen silent what with the exertions of the past half-hour, and slumps herself sofa-wise as I scan the terminal and sort the dross from the needed and relevant.

~ What do you want munch-wise? Danny calls through.

I haven't even thought about food since morning. She must be hungry herself, else wouldn't bother asking.

~ Just call down for some boxes and stick them on the tab, I call, and the immediate bulky shifting tells me that she needs no persuasion.

Mum sounds happy enough on audio. She never uses the screen, not happy to face the device unless well made-up and groomed.

~ Francine, it's Mum here. Hello. Ehm, you not there? Eh? No? Alright, well, ehm, it's just to let you know I'm fine and I might be coming up for a few days, maybe the Bank Holiday Monday, so I might have to crash if that's alright. Alright? Okay dear, bye now, take care.

So that's it. The usual. Mum calls every month or thenabouts, and it's usually the same message – I'm coming up, okay if I crash? And then she never does. Can't blame her really. She probably does feel guilty for leaving, what with me still so young and all that, but the job she's got is a good one, supposedly, and there wasn't much doing here unless you want to stack shelves or talk to strangers on the phone all day. She works just the four days and clears two and a half so that's quite good, if it's true.

Someone said to Kelly one day down at the Depot that my Mum's doing the streets in Manchester or some such dive, and when she told me I went storming off with steaming ears and dragged out this blue-haired yapper from the pee-oh where, like so many of her age, she seems to live, and she was kicking and screaming and her pish was spattering on the paving but I was ready to give her what-for even if she was like about ninety-five and she points out this guy standing with his buddies over outside the bookies, croaks that he told her, so she's dropped and I'm after him then, and after a short run I have him up against the wall at the back of the telly-shop and I'm just about to remove his jarlers bare-handed when he starts blabbing and giving it serious gush, and it dawns on me that this sad specimen can't be more than first year at the General, so I drop him as he assures me that he doesn't even know me or my Mum, and he only said it cos he heard someone else at school say it about Bulletproof Suzy's Mum, so I feel sorry for him and let him go on his way, and that was really that, but I know they still talk.

Looking at it calmly now I suppose it's all quite possible, and no great surprise if it was, truth be told, what with Mum still being only thirty-three and a good looker, for all the difference that would make I suppose. But it does hurt a tad to ponder my very own Mum doing pretty much the same as me, that is screwing people for cash – she should be inside at night watching the flickers and relaxing, not traipsing wet streets at the mercy of night-plodding scabbers and pervoids. Her choice anyway, and whenever I do ask her about work she just says that the office is nice and she's doing ever so well, but no I can't call her there 'cos it's too busy and she'd get shit for it and besides, she prefers to hear from me when she's at home and she can relax with a cup of tea, this being Mum's nickname for a very large voddy with bitter lemon.

I web into the CO's central site and run up the daily details onscreen. Nothing done, so it's a row of solid zeros. I can do this with my eyes shut now. I do a quick check on the averages. Despite the fruitless last couple of days we're still well up for the month, and even with these two consecutive blanks it'll take the office a few days to register it and get in touch to find out what the problem is, so I stare at the figures and the bleeping blanks and wonder if maybe now I should try to think about Joanne and her killer or killers, and what, if anything, I'm going to do about it all.

I haven't been able to talk to anyone about it. Couldn't talk to my little ladies 'cos they don't want to see me greeting and confused and asking for advice or sympathy. I'm their boss, I'm in charge, and I can't and won't let anything get in the way or wear that down. The instant I lose authority, it's over, and if I can only keep it together for another five or six months I'll have enough to get out and away for good. The brochures I got from the agents are all in a shoe box way up the back of my wardrobe, and I only ever take it out if I know I've got some time undisturbed. And the travel guides for Spain and Turkey and Italy are well-thumbed now. Just another wee while and I'll have enough to fuck off for a year or two, maybe get a quiet job some-where nice, relax and get a decent tan, maybe even eat what I want when I want and to hell with weight-watching and training. I'll learn how to be nice to myself. That's what they're always on about on the daytime chat shows and the phone-ins. Getting in touch with yourself, realising that you are what you are and to just accept it, all that sort of gumphiness. I can't take it seriously long enough to ponder that there might be something in it.

But the pain which sweeps through me when I realise how selfish I am is a terrible thing. Maybe it's just guilt, I don't know, but it starts right inside my guts and makes me want to chuck-up. Mum leaving? Who could blame her with me always in bother and not even trying to get a job and just generally being a bit of a let-down. Dad leaving, wrecked with booze, and never coming back? Said he couldn't handle me, the responsibility, the pressure. I must've been a right handful to make a big man like that crack and run helter-skelter for his sanity. And now Joanne dead, and right outside my house? Who will say it's all coincidence?

And here I sit not twenty-four hours after seeing her propped against that lamp-post, and maybe she was still warm, and what did I do? I pulled my woolly cap lower and sauntered past the growing crowd of gabbing rubberneckers and went straight to my flat knowing full well it was her. Maybe I secretly thought the rozz would come straight up. Maybe I expected that the Whammer and the Flash would wear off and I'd sleep like a baby and next day I would find a clean rain-washed pavement where the apparition had been. Or maybe I just turned my head from my dead friend cos she hadn't been quite as good a friend as I'd wanted her to be, and now she was dead she was fuck all good at all. Worse, she was dead at my front door and liable to cause me much rozz-entanglement as well as grief.

I know I must still be in a form of shock, but there's no way I'm going to any casualty or doc. It's a matter of time before they take me in. They were up earlier. They'll be back.

The boxes arrive from Ollie's on the second floor, steaming hot and wafting hungry smells all through the flat. We sit afront the vidder and quietly pig, watching the omnibus edition of Danny's favoured soap she's taped. It's the usual tosh, the old familiar faces still careering about, bickering and fighting without ever swearing, scrapping with no real harm being done, getting weepy and hyper and philosophical just in time for the ad breaks to find some way of keeping the whole thing hanging till the next exciting chunk. Still, we nearly always watch them when we're munching. It's like seeing normal lives, even though we know they're anything but. Maybe we wish they were.

I'm lobbing my gear into the laundro and intending to hit the shower when Danny calls through. I go into the telly room expecting to find her stretched out on the sofa, but she's at the window, looking down at Magenta entrance, and she pulls the curtain back a tad then peers over at the footbridge and the brewery-path, dark and quiet now we're past midnight.

~ Suzy, did you recognise any of them? she asks, and I'm pretty taken aback given that Danny is not the sort to ask questions of any sort regarding anything bar food and soaps and other stimulants.

I know I had that feeling about the leader, but I haven't cracked a light to Danny so far.

~ Did you? I ask, and Danny turns to me then, and rarely have I seen her look so deep in thought.

~ Well, I'm not sure. You know that guy Joanne was seeing? she asks then, and I take a seat, wondering where this is all leading.

~ Bobby Harris?

~ Right. Bobby. Did he have a beard that guy? Danny says before sinking into the armchair opposite me and pulling her jacket over her shoulders.

~ Well, if you could call it such. A bum-fluff effort, and sideys. His hair's long, big chunky straggles like he's trying to grow dreads but can't get them started. What about him anyway?

~ I think he was there, Danny says, and my incredulous smile doesn't affect her.

~ I couldn't swear to it, but see when they were lined up and that madwoman was dancing and jumping at us? I caught one of them, right at the far left end. He was kind of hiding I'd say, behind his bigger chums. None of the rest of them was behind anyone. They were all standing neat as you like in a big line. But not him. I'm sure it was him. I'm not at it, honest.

There seems no obvious reason why Danny would lie about such a sighting, real or imagined. But Bobby running with the Shaws? Too crazy to contemplate. Bobby's from Mayhill, and you can't get much further from the South and still be in the same city. It just doesn't make any sense, but I keep the reservations to myself.

~ What about that lass? I ask, and Danny laughs one of her tinny, nervous laughs.

~ It's that way now I'm getting mixed-up and starting to think I might've, but, no, no way, I wouldn't forget a coupon like that. Did you see that scar? Mental case.

Bobby? If it was him, he's taking his life in his hands. The Mayhill teams, which vary in size and reputation, have a combined membership running into four figures. There's no other area in the city with so many well-known squads, and if Bobby, who was certainly brought up here, is moving by night with Southsiders then he must have a very good reason or else has taken leave of whatever marbles he may have had. In any event, Bobby was never known as a wannabe, never aspired to ticketdom. Joanne told me once that he was well into the animal rights and the anti-roads stuff, and apart from the very occasional bout of rozz-bashing, they're not really regarded as serious street contenders.

But Danny seems genuine enough, and she has to be credited with a good memory for the old visages, so I make a mental note to trace the whereabouts of young Bobby Harris with a view to having a quiet word, then leave Danny to resume watching the story of ordinary folk down Southways, and buzz down to Kieran.

~ Did those rozz state their origin? I ask.

He ruffles paper.

~ Yeah. Spring Central, he replies.

Right then. That'll be a start. First thing tomorrow, down to Spring Central. They'll have their version of what happened, and I'd best find out how it is that I fit into their view of it all. If they're going to keep coming here looking for me I'm as well going to them. That's taking initiative. That's wrong-footing your opponent.

Well, that's the theory.

CHAPTER FIVE

It takes an age to drop off that night. Twice I'm up telling Danny to turn down the audio on the vidder, and the second time she shifts her chair right up to the box, making to plug her earholes into the headers.

But I know it's not the telly keeping me awake. Maybe it was like shock wearing off or that, but it was finally sinking in that Joanne was dead and gone forever, and every time my peepers shut I was getting like highlights of our friendship, wee bits and bobs, things that lingered inside my nog, like snippets of a film whose story you can't remember even though you know for fact you've seen it maybe three or four times.

Trying not to think about her as she looked propped up against the lamp-post makes me think of how she looked when she was alive, and it's upsetting how difficult it is to see her face still, to see individual features. If you ask me to describe her nose without the rest of her, I can't. I can't say that her chin was like this or her ears were like that, it wouldn't make sense. She was all in a one-er, and I can't think of her any other way. It's like I can only remember her face in motion, along with her voice and her walk.

And it seems like every snippet of conversation that comes back now is like niggardly wee snidey arguments about pure and utter trivia, like I was always trying to make out that she was wrong and daft and being naïve when most of the time I knew full well that she was absolutely right, and she knew I knew. But maybe it was just her way of winding me up and getting me to use the brain she was always saying that I have, 'cos when I think of it now it always ended up that she would give in and let me win, but five minutes later she'd be on about something else and I would still be trying to figure out how she didn't mind losing an argument, and double-checking what she'd actually said. But I feel truly wretched and gnarly now to think of my grumpiness with her, as patient as she was. Why couldn't I have been happier with her, made more of an effort to enjoy her way of looking at things and try agreeing with her for once?

I can't even remember the first time we met. Not clearly, like it was some Robin Hood and Little John type confrontation, 'cos it wasn't like that at all. She was in my school when we were about ten or thereabouts, but she was always hanging about with Julie and Misha and all that crowd, whereas I was very much for keeping on my todsome, especially at the playtimes, when I'd be offsky playing like Bulldogs and stuff with the guys.

She was quite cool in a quietish way, and although she was pretty smart, always up there getting like third prizes or whatever, she never made much of a deal of it as do some. And 'cos she was that bit higher in the class I never really got to sit anywhere near her either, as she was on the long new desk at the very back of the class with sundry other bright young things and I was right down there on my own in front of old Budgie's desk where she could keep her watery stroke-damaged eye on me. So that was two years in the wee school that me and Joanne Friel were in the same class, and I can't remember one conversation from that whole time.

She was very good at painting and drawing and all that sort of stuff, and she liked doing copies of cartoon characters and pop favourites, movie starlets etc. Budgie didn't approve of such silliness so Joanne would carry her drawings and stuff about with her in her bag and we'd sometimes get a look if it wasn't raining. Misha and Julie use to get her to do like poster-sized drawings of The Five Jimmys and Todd Franko and sundry other heart-throbbers, but I never ever got the courage up to ask her to do one for me of the Pandabashers, in whose fan club I was member four hundred and eighty three.

Plus she was pretty good at the sporty side of stuff, and that's likely why I didn't really get onto her as much as I did some of the others. Not that I was scared of her mind, but I suppose I had a sort of admiration for her, wishing I could run as fast and not be quite so heavy and slow as I was. She wasn't ever really the prettiest in the class either, but she was always neat and clean and walked nice, and sometimes I would watch her in the playground, just as she was walking about, and I would watch that walk very carefully and try to copy it when school was over and I was making the long and boring plod homebound.

I loved her hair. Mine has always been poker-straight and was blonde when I was wee, but got mousier as the years went on and was like mucky-puddle brown by the first year of General High, flat and stuck to my scalp and as lifeless as can be. But Joanne had this fabulous gleaming blonde hair with like faint strawberry tints in it, purely natural of course, and it was so curly and wavy that it was different every day, and even different from morning to evening depending on the weather. If her hair got wet and dried naturally, it almost curled in front of you as you watched, and would become a snarly web of like sparkling goldiness. I've got a post-card of a drawing of an angel by Leonardo or somesuch wonderman, and it's exactly what Joanne's hair was like. But she preferred it straighter, and would pick and pull at it when it went too tight until she got it streaming down in like springy curls.

I wanted my hair like hers so much that I once bought a dye in the first year of General and set about it, but I got fed-up trying to pull my hair through this tight plastic bunnet with this dead sharp crochet-hook type implement, and eventually just whapped the whole bowlful right on my skull and rubbed it all in. I can still remember watching it change colour in the mirror, and panicking when I heard the key going and I knew it was Mum, so I rinsed out the whole lot as fast as I could and made for my room, and when it was dry it was white and gold and canary-yellow and streaks of brown and rusty red and a thousand other shades between brown and red and yellow and white and it was like an old style carpet. I had to have it done completely bleached then, and shaved down to get the burned bits out, and with the terrible beasting I then took at the hands of older General High students, as well as anyone else who happened to glimpse me unbunneted in the street, I became mowlier and snarlier than ever and really started getting naughty.

It was really that first year of General that we became friends. No-one wanted to start at the Nex, this being the nickname given to the arrangement of like drab bungalow efforts painted innards-pink which acted as a supposedly temporary annexe to the main Gen, but had been in constant use since being converted from a prisoner of war station in the last big war, and as if to leave proof for further generations who might be sceptical, the barbed wire was still curled rusty atop the huge chicken wire fencing which enclosed the compound.

So I've stayed late on this Monday to test for the school karate team. I'm still under five feet at the time, being slow and late on the physical development side of things, but I've been banging away on my own wee punch-bag in the house for a few weeks and doing like stretching exercises on my legs every morning before school, hoping that this might help them to get longer so that I'll be tall and straight and lean, like Joanne. Mum's always been quite keen for me to try and get into this team, the Nex being well-served for facilities what with a small gymnasium in one of the prefabs, and a fair selection of equipment for general use, cos she feels it'll help me confidence-wise and perhaps draw me out of what she calls my like shell.

It's a warmish evening, must be Autumn early-time, and the sun is shielded with this sort of haze. I always run from the school until I get to the path leading by the playing fields, 'cos that's where you can pretty much see for a good bit in all directions, so if any team does come a-running with a view to plunder, you have options escape-wise. Over the Rex, these being the ashy recreation grounds, mostly football fields, and then it's another five minutes hoof over the footbridge to Viewhill, then home is barely a minute's hard sprint if it comes to it.

It's very still this evening, and barely a body about what with it being after six. So the test has gone alright, I think, and the teacher – this great big thin woman called Miss Wilko – had actually asked me to stay with a smaller group after letting some of the others go home, and she asked me to demonstrate my punching a couple of times on big fat red mitts that she slipped over her hands. It felt great to punch something other than the bag, something that had a mind behind it, and I didn't hold back, much to her initial surprise and admiration. She had a couple of the fifth and sixth year students there too to show us what they could do, and they were stretching into unusual shapes and going through these set movements which were more sort of ballet than fighting for my liking, but all in all it was great and I can't wait to go back again and just pray and hope that Mum will be able to afford to get me the gear.

With it being quiet on the path, and feeling more than a smidgeon knacked after the exertion of it all, I don't run as per usual, but plod happy and steady and enjoy the coolness of the sweat drying on my back as I proceed. I'm just turning the corner which leads up to the car entrance to the Rex when I see this crowd a good bit further up, right by the fence.

It's three lassies from the year above me, and they've got this other lass against the wire fence. The tallest of these is going through the girl's pockets as the other two hold her arms, laughing and putting their faces right up to hers and generally terrorising her.

I duck back around the corner, where the fence actually starts, and wait. If I make a detour up by the canal I can eventually work my way back down to the Cerulean footbridge and thence home, but that's maybe another half hour and Mum's already expecting me back for dinner.

Then the girl must make a bid of sorts for freedom, or else the big lass decides to have a bit of a lark with her 'cos the fence suddenly starts shaking. It's one of those tall wirey fences, like massive chicken-wire, and the whole length of it is like one piece held upright by iron poles. So this small shriek rings out plaintive and kind of scary. I stick my napper round the corner and see that the victim has managed to get herself on top of the tallest lassie and that's when I realise it's Joanne who's being given the hard time.

I drop my bag at the corner, and although they're still a good fifty yards away, I'm only about twenty feet away when they finally notice me. By this time Joanne's got the big one on the deck and she's got one of her knees pinning down an arm and she's like leathering slaps all over the lassie's face, and it's her shrieking I've heard. The other two stand back and are giving real hard like toe-kicks into Joanne, even trying to get her head, but it's like she's possessed or something and she doesn't even notice, just keeps pummelling like mad at this squalling bully below.

I go in feet first at the one with her back to me, and she goes spinning right over the fighting couple and ends up decked beside her pal, and as the friend moves back, giving it palms up and all angel eyes, I crack her one on the chin and she hops way back pronto. Then I have to haul Joanne off the bloodied bully leader, and even when I've got her up on her feet she's still snarling and like foaming, and her eyes are riveted on this dishevelled bully and she wants back to give her more. Her knuckles are split and bleeding, and I'm not surprised to see that the gangly wheezing coughing lass has a black gap where previously she must have had a tooth.

As I hold Joanne, trying to calm her and telling her it's alright, the leader sees the chance to escape, and she does a sort of backwards crab-football thing before scrambling onto her hands, and knees, then getting up with great shakiness and the much-needed assistance of both friends. The three line up and sort of face us and I'm pretty sure we're about to start round two, but I can see that the biggest one knows full well she has me to thank for retaining ownership of the rest of her teeth, and Joanne is still tugging and jerking and looks mad enough to carry on where she left off, so they turn, move away, pausing only to issue a couple of warnings, but then the big one starts crying, perhaps having realised that her dental arrangement has been changed, and her pals comfort her as they head off back the way I just came.

Joanne is white as a scared sheet with the shock and adrenalin no doubt, so I say I'll see her home if she likes and she sort of mumbles she's alright, and thanks anyroad, but when she starts shuffling off without even picking up her various bits and bobs I realise that she's in quite a bad way so I call her back and we get her stuff back into her pockets and her backsack and I walk with her up to the bus stop.

It's a fair old distance too to where she lives, and thankfully she has enough to cover the fares, me being rooked as per usual, but best to stick with her as she really does look on the point of keeling over, and if I leave her now here might be recriminations and such should more damage befall her on her lonesome.

As soon as we get to her house – very neat new brick-work and white windows etc. – I ask her mum if it's okay for me to call my mum, and that's cool. It takes ages for her to pick-up, engrossed as she surely is in one of the never-ending discussion progs she favours as her daytime viewing, and when I tell here where I am and what happened she doesn't sound mightily bothered and says she'll stick something in the micro for me to get later, and that's that. Joanne's mum is all sweetness and smiles and thank-you-so-much and here's-a-cuppa and you'll-stay-for-your-tea and all that so I say thanks very much, that would be nice, nice and proper as one is supposed to, and I'm taken up to Joanne's room and told to make myself comfortable while Joanne is much fussed over and a phone call is made, maybe to the local rozz-shop.

Joanne's room is something else – first floor, view onto the garden and the canal on the other side of the low wall, and even a couple of swans gliding past as the sun goes down behind my own Viewhill block in the distance and it's like something off a postcard, or the pictures that flash past at the start of the holiday prog.

She also has the very latest by way of complete info-tainment, with the telly and radio and CD and PC and phone all boxed black and silver and neatly slotted into this like custom-made bookshelf arrangement. It is the very latest and chicest of set-ups, and well-impressed I must look when Joanne comes in, still a tad wobbly-looking, but at least with a bit of pinkness back on her face after having had her minor cuts and grazes attended to and smeared with some highly pungent cleansing lotion.

She's understandably droopy, and sort of slumps on the bed with much puffing and slight sighs of like pain and strain, so I ask her if she wants me to go and let her have a kip and she's all no, no, no, you must stay 'cos Mum's making dinner for you and all that, so I'm quite pleased truth be told.

She asks me if I want to play her new vidder game, but I ask her if I can see her infotainment set-up on the go and she's very happy to tell me how to get it on, and it's amazing right enough. It's pretty much the same as we got a couple of times at the Nex, the main difference being that there isn't a squad of like forty sprogs all waiting turns, so you can actually get your hands on it and do what you want rather than plodding through some pre-set boredom, and she shows me the webs and the net-nests and all sorts, the mail she's got going with folks all over, in Africa and Russia as was, and even in Australia. She starts showing me some magazines about the programming and all that sort of stuff and it seems that she's well into it, but I can't keep up with what she's on about and the stuff in the mags looks very dry and maths-like to me and I think she susses that I'm rather clueless about such material and so she eventually just goes back to showing me the easier stuff.

It feels like a few minutes before her old dear gives it rap-a-rap on the door and Joanne makes a painful rise to her feet and we go to the kitchen-diner room where there is no telly and all the grub is spread across this big table and the other sprogs have already taken their seats.

The dinner itself is a grand affair, or so it seems to me, with authentic meat, stringy and very soft, accompanied by like piles of steaming vegetables and spuds of both boiled and roasted variety, this massive plateful followed by an apple-crumble-type sweet of home-made ilk covered with this shiny red sauce, and there's a glass of flavoured milk, raspberry if I recall right. So what a belly-full I have there, not wanting to let Joanne down or make her mum feel bad by leaving even the tiniest scrap of anything on any of the plates put afront me. The whole thing makes me think of Christmas as seen on the box.

Joanne also has the two younger brothers, who stay quiet throughout the meal and leave as soon as granted permission. It seems that they were not normally so mellow, and that my presence had something to do with it. The older sister, who was not present, was working in Hong Kong or Japan or somesuch similarly far-flung Eastern zone, and was doing missionary work with their dad. Pictures are produced from shelves and cabinet drawers, and her dad's a jolly looking soul, very tall with pure beaming smile, standing in front of this or other famous landmark, sometimes with the daughter, sometimes on his todsome, and sometimes with huge crowds of like students or congregation, whatever they might be, but all happiness and sun and very exotic altogether. Joanne tells me that he's been doing it for twenty years and she hardly ever sees him, but that's on account of her mum not having any urge to pursue the calling, whatever that is.

Still, even with talk of God and a multitude of dodgy

questions from her mum about my own family, it's a brilliant evening capped off in some style when we're back in Joanne's room listening to the new Mitchell Brothers CD, and the door gets rap-a-rapped again and this time her mum sticks her head in and says that's the taxi waiting, and I'm about to ask Joanne where she's going when she looks at my face and laughs and explains that it's for me, and by the time I get in it's almost ten, and Mum's asleep on the couch.

So we're friends from then on I suppose. Usually, I'm up to hers after school, and some nights I'll stay over if it's coming to the week-end. I start doing homework so I can stay while she's doing hers. Come to think of it, that was probably the first year I ever went into any exam period knowing roughly what was going on.

I think she liked having me about, especially when we went out. She wasn't as wary and quiet when I was with her, not that she had much cause to be scared anyway. But I don't think she knew what she was capable of, and so I managed to persuade her to come up to mine and she had a go at the bag and started practising some basic moves. She was a bit scared of it in the sense that if her mum found out she said she'd be in real trouble. But her mum never did find out, not from me at any rate, and she came up to Viewhill regular, usually on Saturday afternoons, and we'd have a couple of hours doing reps and bag-work and occasionally some light weights. And she learned fast.

Yeah, she learned really fast. For all the bastarding good it ended up doing her. Awake again. I haven't even contacted her folks. Her dad and sister will no doubt be on their way back home for the funeral, gushing quietly on a plane somewhere high over some part of the world between here and there, wondering why and how and who and where and all that, and even I, here, have to ask the same questions, and the only ones I really don't know, the ones I really have to know, are the who and the why.

I have to kind of shove my face right deep into the pillow to try and drown out the miserable mewly sobbing sounds that are coming from way down in my stomach lest Danny hear and try to investigate.

And the worst thing about it all is that we kind of stopped seeing each other the instant I started as L.O. So I bumped into her a couple of times down at The Depot, usually when she was going to and from the library, but even though I always waved or whistled across and she always acknowledged, we never really got back to proper talking terms.

Not that I thought it was all over. I figured she was still just in some sort of major bad mood and would eventually come round, let us agree to disagree about the whole thing. And I suppose I was so busy with the work that I was hardly getting any time to make the call or the visit that might kick start it all again and give us a chance to get it back to where it was. But the excuses, 'cos that's what I know they are, they start the pathetic wailing up again and I grit my teeth and curse myself and the Commissioner's Office and everyone and anything else that comes to mind, knowing full well that I'm as much to blame as anyone.

The night goes on, and it's one of those where no real sleep is had, all half-dreams and real noises mixing with the imagined and making pictures from smells and movements, and maybe it's the moderate intake of

White Flash that evening, or maybe the joint, then the spectacle of the Shaws confronting us on our own door, but the whole night becomes a series of stuttering night-mares where I'm seeing Joanne alive and happy, and Mum in her usual smiley photo-pose, and then Mum's face is on Joanne's body, half propped up against the lamp post, with like black jelly hanging out of one eye and the other staring at nothing, her neck gaping like a new and extra-big mouth. It won't go away.

It's before dawn when I get up, shower, dress in plain dullness and breakfast on porridge and bananas. Before nine I'm out of Magenta and hoofing it to Spring Central. I have to find out. No more work, no more to do with my little ladies or anyone else until I know what happened, and if I play my cards right I'm pretty sure the rozz will tell me what they know.

CHAPTER SIX

~ You'll just have to come back later, the desk-rozz says, tapping her pen on the metal bit of the clipboard, the officer dealing with the case won't be back till midday at the very earliest.

~ I'll wait then, I say, but calm and polite as you like, and then half-camp myself in the broom cupboard making like a waiting room.

There's a totally stinking old dear sitting half-asleep by the radiator, and it's impossible to sit on the only other available seat, which happens to be beside her, without getting serious dry boak, and even when I try to move the chair it gives out a loud and alarming squarking noise, being firmly bolted to the deck, and the old dear is thus aroused from her stinking slumber and fires me a look of fear and warning.

I squat down by the doorway, which does not actually have a door, and watch the rozz plod in and out and in and out, on and off their shifts, meeting the occasional glance of recognition with my customary bold stare and sarky grin, but I'm forced to venture out into the cold and frosty morning from time to time when the stench of the snoozing crumbly old boiler monopolises all available fresh air and unconsciousness looms.

Three hours of this like nose-hell pass before Yardley comes in. He was the Community Plod for Viewhill before the post was scrapped, and he knows me, well, knows of me. He kind of pauses at the doorway, coughs a little as the wall of salty rancidness swoops up his nostrils, and puts his working frown back on before addressing me in the sort of tone which might normally start me mowling and snorting, but not this morning.

~ Brallahan. Nice of you to show up, he says, but you can tell that he's starting to take the heave of dry variety and the smell is making his eyes water, so he backs off into the corridor and I follow.

~ You're Officer Yardley, am I not right? say I, and he coughs yes.

He's setting a pretty brisk pace down the corridor, and we turn to the left and to the right, and he's nodding at these passing plain clothes rozz and it's all very fast and urgent and serious, just like you see in the heavier rozz flicks, and for a half-second I imagine that I wouldn't mind working in somewhere like this, 'cos what they can do is march about looking serious and troubled by what they've seen and heard in all their eventful years as rozzloiderlings of various ranks, but for all anyone knows they just march about in here all day, looking troubled and serious and pensive about what they may well have seen and heard, but they see and hear no more, finding it safer to keep going round and round and exchanging meaningful nods and other physical acknowledgments with others who are taking other circuitous routes. Maybe that's why almost every rozz who's ever seen outside the station is almost ages with me – the older, wiser ones, all pensive and troubled with what they've seen and heard, they stay well inside and cannot be removed without wild horse assistance, or at least the promise of some good freebies.

So we eventually come to a door and he shoves it open and stands, allowing me to enter, and there's a small table, two chairs facing across it, and I take the one that's got a better view of the door, but I've no sooner parked my fundament than a very crude thumb-jerk indicates that I called it wrong and must shift, which I do, still smiling and being ever so demure all the while.

The room is only marginally easier on the nasal senses than the waiting room, there being a fierce blend of strong antiseptic and a half-a-million or so high-tar fags, and the No Smoking sign itself bears the kind of brown varnish normally only ever seen in very old-style pubs. Seems that Officer Yardley isn't exactly rolling out the red carpet for me.

He sits down with a sigh and another little cough, probably still tasting the hellish aroma of the waiting room squatter. He very carefully moves a big blue rubber band from a scabby paper folder and carefully opens it. I notice that his fingers shake just a little. He's got nice hands, much nicer than mine, clean straight nails finely cut, and very young looking compared to his face, which suggests his age at somewhere between thirty and forty. He's not in the least bit intimidating, although I rather fancy that he thinks he is, and the frown he wears to confirm his authority looks a tad out of place, as if he's maybe just borrowed it from someone else for the morning, or else there are only so many of them in stock and he has to sign it in and out every day.

~ Right, he says, and looks at me, shifting slightly forward.

I smile broader, trying to look pleasant and up for a right good gab on any subject he desires.

~ Right, I say.

He shifts the top papers slightly apart, then pushes them together again and looks back up.

~ If you don't mind my saying, it's a bit unusual.

~ What is? I reply.

~ You coming in, he says, it's unusual.

~ Well, being a responsible citizen and all that, I heard that you sent some of your boys up to see me and I wasn't there, so figured I should do the decent thing and return the compliment. It's nice to be nice and all that, I say, smiling still and quite relaxed if you please, sitting back as far as the grotty metal chair will allow and one leg raised and comfily folded across the other knee.

~ That's very decent indeed. Very responsible, he says, and he's looking at the papers.

I get a wee bit of a start when the door opens, but it's clear that this is what was putting Yardley a tad on edge, and I realise now he didn't like being alone with me. He's scared of me. He gets up and has a quick handshake with the large man who enters. I haven't seen him before.

~ Suzy, says Yardley, this is John Ross. Inspector John Ross. He's leading the investigation.

~ Nice to meet you, Inspector. And what investigation

are you in charge of then? I ask, deliberately making myself look and sound as naïve as is possible.

Yardley scowls at me, but the big fellow laughs, and quite an infectious, genuine guffaw it is too.

~ Ah, you are Francine, he says, and that accent's just a mite unusual, first impression suggesting he hails from the distant North, perhaps even as far as Inverness or thereabouts.

~ Francine, yes, but I'm sure Steven here has been referring to me by my local nomiker, which happens to be Suzy.

~ Yes indeed, says the big fellow, hands in pockets, head bowed as he paces to the far and rather gloomy corner where there is a low shelf, a power point, and nothing else.

He leans against the wall by the shelf. Yardley gets a pen out and scribbles something on the pad he's taken from the folder, but he's sitting back now and has propped the folder against the table edge so that I can see neither what he's writing nor what other papers he shuffles through as his big colleague takes the reins.

~ It's nice you popping in like this, he says, still a trace of a laugh in his tone, because I'm actually just off the phone there, talking to the Commissioner's Office trying to get hold of your details.

~ I don't suppose they were very helpful then? I venture, and he folds his arms and makes this like extremely fake and melodramatic frown.

~ Oh no, no, no. Not very helpful at all, and I'm sure you'd be rather worried if they were wouldn't you? he says, and I get a fleeting tingle now of what this guy is capable of and what he's up to, he surely knowing just as well as I that the Commissioner's Office is bound not to disclose any information about its staff via telephone or other electronic or written media to anyone, even the police or other local authorities, without written permission to do so.

~ I'm glad to hear it, I say, and I slow down a little and try to choose my words like careful.

~ Oh, I didn't tell you, but the investigation I'm in charge of relates to a friend of yours, he says then, and he walks over a bit closer, standing behind Yardley.

~ Joanne, I say.

~ Yes, Joanne. Joanne Friel, says Ross, and he leans over Yardley and plucks a sheet from the folder and slides it across the table towards me.

Even with the picture upside-down, it's instantly recognisable, and tallies pretty much exactly with my Flash-befuddled memory of the scene, albeit from a slightly more elevated angle and much more brightly lit.

This guy Ross moves right up to the table, and turns the picture very slowly so I'm seeing it the right way up, and I can feel his eyes and those of his younger colleague boring into me looking for whatever reaction. No point trying to act, pretend. I know the pain must show.

~ She was a good friend? asks Ross, and I nod dumbly.

Ross starts walking back to his corner, and when I look at Yardley he looks away.

~ Not what we heard, Suzy, says Ross, and he's staring away up at the corner, back facing me.

The inkling of what the guy is capable of becomes a full-fledged shadow with scary pointy bits and a dark growly soundtrack underpinning it, and I know I should shut it and keep it shut but I want so much to get on with it and they can't possibly be serious about starting this stuff.

~ Look, I say, I don't need this shit. You know fine well it wasn't me. Joanne was my friend. My best friend.

~ Like I say, says Ross, that's not what we've heard.

I stand up, mowly with pure rage that he's not facing me when he speaks. I point at him, and I sense Yardley tensing and shifting back in his seat.

~ So what did you hear! comes out as a very loud challenge rather than a question, and Ross turns now and makes his way over fast, also pointing.

~ You will sit down and shut your hole unless I tell you otherwise! he pure roars, and I wait just a tad and stare him out hard before I do, and I can feel the eyes start to widen and my skin drain, but perhaps this is retrievable if I can just cool it.

~ Now, he says, adjusting his cuff and tie as he strolls back to his corner, then back again to the table, let's rewind a bit and do that again. What we've heard is that you had an argument with Joanne a while back. A bad argument. For five years you were like Siamese twins, next thing she's crossing the street you're on. We find her knifed outside your block. Do you seriously think you can sound off about how friendly you were with her after killing her, then expect us to break open a box of tissues?

~ I don't have to answer anything, I say robotic style, and the anger surges up in his voice again.

~ I didn't ask you to answer anything. I'm telling you something. I'm telling you that we've already got six witnesses who have stated that they saw you outside Magenta Court at ten-thirty. Joanne's estimated time of death was ten-thirty to ten-forty five. You were there, she was there, she ends up dead. Now, call me an old fashioned copper, but even someone as dense as this old teuchter can put two and two together. And it's not like I'm even biased Suzy. I mean, I've heard a lot about you and your gang, what you call your little ladies, I've heard about the beatings and the intimidation, the knives, the drugs. I know what you're up to. But even that I can put aside and still say hand on heart that your fingers have that lassie's blood on them and you'll answer for it.

I scan him slow and careful, and mould the look to a softer kittenish style, looking for a response. He's genuinely angry and revolted and outraged if his expression is anything to go by, but with rozzloiders, even the highland-hailing variety, expressions are nothing to go by, and I wonder what his bag is. A boozer? A fire and brimstoner? A mad womaniser who prefers them young? All I can tell from the ferocious contortion of his facial musculature is that he hates me, and that does not make sense, no sense at all.

Anyone who has ever been in a fight knows that anger is a strange thing. Old dears lift up cars to release trapped weans, weakling men manage to drop the mightiest of foes with apparent ease. But anger hardly ever arises from genuine hatred. Anger is hot and jaggy and sharp, whereas real hate is cool, like mercury, and level and strong and cannot be altered or diluted.

Miss Wilko, who tried to teach me karate properly, used to bang on long and hard about the essence of the art and the importance of calm and all that, and it was a subject also most close to Joanne's heart what with her being a pacifist and into non-violent resistance and so on. This side of things has always appeared rather mysterious to me, not because I'm some sort of neanderthal who likes kicking the fuck out of the inno-cent, but because I have never, and still do not understand how it is that people manage to remain calm and peace-focussed when their only clear and sensible option is to put the mitts up and scrap.

It's like when you get these guys up at the park on the Sunday mornings. I've only ever seen it the once, but it's raw fighting between guys for money, and there's no rules. None at all. And more often than not these guys will not be fighting because they have any particular problem with each other. It's not like one has killed the other's granny and is seeking revenge, and the other had every good reason to kill the granny and will fight again to prove his case. They do it because winning gives them power. It's a transaction of sorts, and the guys who stand about them and put bets on and egg them on, they are formal witnesses to it. Of course, the fighters know that full well, and more often than not they probably have a great deal of respect for each other, but when it comes down to that few minutes in the run-up to the actual scrap you can be sure that their minds will be going haywire trying to develop a hatred of the opponent, and the best of these rule-less fighters can switch it on and off, like some folk can cry on cue. They can suddenly make themselves hate the other guy by imagining him to be someone else who has perhaps done them real harm, or imagining that whatever misfortune may have befallen family members or friends is down to this opposite character, and that's when they go off onto another level of violence where they're speedier and much more brutal than they would be if sent into a proper boxing ring with gloves on and all that.

If you can imagine staying up all night getting pished and Whammed and shagged and whatever else you might care to do of a Saturday, then going into the local park and going head to head with some psychopath from the Rucky who's odds-on and has won ten in a row, then you just might get an idea of what it's like to suddenly develop a hate for someone you don't know. You just might.

Cos surely, and I say this after long and weary experience of it all, surely you do not have to hate someone to be able to harm them? Me and the little ladies do it all the time, and we growl and we snarl and we flick open blades and stamp our boots and howl at imaginary moons and generally frighten the wits and shits and all other bits out of pretty much anyone we get hold of. But we don't hate them. To hate someone is to feel strongly about them, and I can't think of anyone at all I really truly hate.

Dad? Sometimes, when I think of Mum maybe being on the game. Joanne? Never, even if she did go and turn her back on me and end up dead as a result. Mum? Used to, but don't all teenagers at some point, and they always grow out of it and realise that it wasn't hate at all.

Yes, this Inspector Ross certainly does hate me, of that I've no doubt, but given that he doesn't know me, it's probably fair to assume that he's got a picture of me from someone or somewhere which has filled him with this hate, and Steven Yardley would seem an obvious suspect, and I look at him afresh.

Nothing new – the same fake frown, the pasty complexion. He fears me, sure, but I doubt he has any real hate in him, and no love either. He's one of those guys who has a mild dislike for everyone, and dislikes some less than others, this latter group probably consisting of relatives, friends, lovers, pets. His life is a great big millstone about his scrawny neck, and if he can get anyone to help him haul it along then he has no qualms about getting it slung about their necks too. It was a typically stupid move to appoint him to the post of Community rozz, and amazing that he lasted two years. In that time he probably did more to incite unrest and general rozz hatred than if they hadn't bothered at all, and it's a testament to his ineptitude and ability to depress anyone who comes near him that the post was eventually scrapped. He looks as if someone has hung him up somewhere dark for a long time and told him every depressing story that was ever told and given him all the downer drugs that it's possible to get, and then they've given him everything he ever wanted and let him have it all for like ten minutes before taking it all away again and saying it was just a joke. He looks dead.

~ This job of yours, pipes up Yardley, and his voice is high and shrill and amazingly irritating just at that point so that I feel like leaning over just a tad and slapping his ear, you're a what-do-you-call-it, a . . .

And he stops then, and I wonder if he's that thick that he can't read or pronounce liaison or what.

~ Liaison Officer I say, still staring at the black and whiteness of poor Joanne.

~ Hard work? he asks then, and my patience goes.

~ Look, am I getting charged with anything, or are you taking my statement or what? I say rapid, and Ross it is who leans down now, quite close so that I get this waft of like some very fruity-style men's perfume, not unpleasant perhaps, but a wee bit too much in this room what with the antiseptic and the old fags and the lingering honk of the stale broom-cupboard still clinging to my nose-walls.

~ You're here of your own accord. You can give your statement now, or wait for legal representation. Your call Suzy, says Ross.

I sit back, take a deep breath to try and get some air of fresh variety and quickly ponder the options. Not a lot.

~ Okay, I'll give my statement now. If it's alright with you chaps I'll call the knowledge and get on the books but I don't have to wait for anyone to be here. I've nothing to hide. And in case you've forgotten, I do have a job and we're really quite busy just now so I'd rather get it all over with.

Ross stands poker-straight, like I've just surprised him. Yardley stares on, and there's a sort of tiredness about his face, like he really can't be bothered with all this. But I'm up for it, and I know that I'll only manage to get anything out of them if I do things their way, and what these rozz most definitely do not like is trying to take statements with legal folk watching. And I'd prefer to do it that way anyroad, 'cos they'll have to tape it all and they'll probably try to give me a hard time before the legal-aid gets here, and if they slip up at all on tape, which is far more likely when no legal beastie is present, then my brief will be able to tear them apart, should it ever come to it.

So there's a fuss about while they get the apparatus sorted, this being a standard tape-deck arrangement, and Yardley fetches me a coffee, and a young female rozz, very neatly dressed in the height of rozz fashion, she comes in and sits by the door, and very pretty she is, but stern and rather annoyed-looking, as if this supervisory task has interrupted a good gab or whatever.

I call the Commissioner's Office from the payphone at the reception, just by the broom-cupboard, and they are pretty helpful after my security's cleared and the call is reverse-charged and put through to their Edinburgh office and a most efficient young man processes my details and says there'll be someone with me soon, but not to give any statement. I tell him I'm going ahead with the statement as I have to get it all over with and have nothing to be worried about, but this he cautions against, urging me to be patient. He says he's going to call Kelly, Kelly and Callaghan right away, and this is also most encouraging, KK&C being by far and away the best defence folk going, so I'm away back into the room, accompanied by Miss Stern-rozz, feeling pretty good about it all and keen to give them what they want so they can reciprocate and give me some inkling cluewise as to what's happening.

Pretty soon, this is maybe half-an hour or so into the statement, I'm in trouble and I know it. It's not that I've been asked much question-wise apart from giving a detailed account of my movements that evening, but in order to give corroboration alibi-wise I quickly have to cite my little ladies, which I know will not go down well with any of them, and may land Gerry in particular in all sorts of bother, and I also have to recount the course we took that evening, the work consisting of eight visits total, three being up the Spring, three in Cerulean, and two in Magenta. All those involved have to be named, and I know this will not impress our clients, no-one wanting to deal with rozz, especially if home-visits of a surprise nature are involved, so I'm sitting back and trying to take stock and wondering if maybe I should just keep my trap firmly shut when Yardley is summoned from the room and comes back in with a very limb-busy and fidgety woman who is my rep, and most unhappy she is with me too, ushering the rozz from the room in brusque style to have a word with me one-to-one like.

So it's a right wrist-slapping then for yours truly, but I hang my head and take it like a professional, aware that I have seriously goofed and am dependent now on this highly-strung middle-aged nanny sort called Miss Angela Warnes.

~ It's not just you I have to look out for here. The Commissioner's Office, as you know, is at the centre of a lot of attention at the moment, and this is precisely the sort of publicity it does not need.

~ But I didn't do it, I say, and she's already shaking her head like she's got fleas before I've even finished saying it.

~ That is not the point, young lady. I'm not particularly worried about what you didn't do, I'm more concerned with what you do do, on a day-to-day basis. And coming here to give a statement is the height of folly. Didn't you read your manual? she says, genuinely distressed and amazed looking in equal measure.

I suppose I go sort of huffy then, embarrassed a tad that I don't know what she's on about, but presumably there must be some gumph in all the material that was sent when I signed up with the CO's that pertains to dealing with rozz and charges and legal processes and suchlike.

She quickly consults a small electronic notebook-type

thing and then takes her specs off and fixes me with a teachery stare.

~ You'll leave with me. I have a case this afternoon which is likely to drag on into tomorrow, that takes us into the week-end, so there's a bit of time to get this together. When you give your statement, it will be on our terms, and on our territory, just as it should have been from the start. Make no mistake about it, Francine, these people want a scalp. I've already been told by people who know a lot more about this than you or me that they will get a result on this, and if they have to resort to creative methods then they will most certainly do so. Do not, I repeat, do not contact anyone, do not speak to anyone, and remove yourself from your current address as soon as possible, preferably this afternoon. Do you have somewhere else you can stay, at least until next week?

This is all a bit heavy and fast for my liking.

~ I'm not sure, well, no, I'm alright. There is somewhere.

She puts the gregs back on, consults her wee calculator thing, and writes a number on her personal name card.

~ This gentleman will help. Call him anytime. If you need to move personal effects, if you need cash, transport, whatever. He will have been informed by now that you will be in touch, so do not hesitate to use him if need be. Now, I really do have to leave. Remember, Francine, remember what I've told you. You are in a very serious situation. I know you didn't kill this girl. I believe you. But whether or not you did isn't really relevant. Come on.

So that's it. She's up and off and I'm trailing after her,

and the stern-faced female rozz who was stationed outside the door sort of trots along with us, gets ahead, and by the time we get to the reception area Yardley has been dragged from wherever, and the big fellow Ross is close behind.

~ Just a second, Miss Warnes, Yardley starts, but it's as the proverbial red rag, and she turns on her shiny heel and raises a small but very rigid and threatening finger towards him and his larger colleague.

~ My client is leaving with me, and she is to be left well and truly alone until I can arrange a time for her to give her statement in full. I sincerely hope that neither of you have any intention, however slight, of trying to contact her in any form except through me, and if you do, I warn you now, the consequences will be deeply unpleasant. My client is barely eighteen years old, is traumatised by the death of her friend, and is in no fit state to suffer the kind of interrogation I know you were putting her through. I would expect this kind of tawdry behaviour from amateurs or incompetents, but to see it among so-called professionals is quite nauseating. Officer Yardley, you can expect to be hearing from the Commissioner's Office directly. And as for you, Inspector, I think it fair to say that your Granton Club application will be on hold for quite a while yet. Good day gentlemen.

She marches on again and we pass the broom-cupboard where the rancid boiler still kips peacefully, then we're out into dazzling sunlight, the sky as blue as a med-sea picture, and great wavy ribbons of cloud snaking down towards Viewhill and home. Miss Warnes marches off towards the car park and I'm still with her as she climbs in to the shiny burgundy Merc.

~ Can I drop you? she asks, and I shake the noggin.

She's about to shut the door when I put my hand on the edge of it, not holding it like, but she gives me a snarly wee look like she thinks I might be out of order.

~ Can I ask a question? I say, and she sort of glances away, maybe embarrassed by the haste she's showing.

~ Of course. You're my client. You can ask whatever you like.

~ How did you know all that stuff back there?

She squints in the sun.

~ Stuff ?

~ About Ross, that application for a club and all that. Do you know him?

She smiles, but it's sort of gnarled and guarded.

~ It's my job to know about people, and what I don't know, I find out. Call the number I gave you, make sure you leave a contact number when you move. I'll be in touch.

I take my hand away and she shuts the expensive-sounding door. I stand back, turn to follow her gaze and see Ross standing at a window, hands in pockets and grim of face, having a good stare. The engine's running. The window buzzes fully down and Miss Warnes has put on a very nice pair of shades.

~ Be careful, Francine, she says, and she gives me a right creepy two-second look, maybe creepier 'cos I can't see it 'cos of the specs, and then she's off, and I turn away from the station and look at Viewhill's sparkling windows and feel Ross staring from his window, and I'm playing with the card in my pocket and I look up at the white clouds and feel small and lost and know not where to go or what to cock-a-doodle.

CHAPTER SEVEN

It's gone mid-day when I get back, and Danny is up and washed and sitting afront the box yet again, dressing-gown on, hair wrapped up in one of my good blue towels, stuffing her great gob with big thick slices of holy ghost and jam, this being her long-established manner of breaking fast.

~ Hurry up and get ready will you, I say, not in the best of moods as she can easily tell.

~ Where did you get to then? she asks, so I give her a swift run down, and it's the first that any of the little ladies has heard mention of the Shaws, and she stuffs and chews all the while and her eyes get bigger and wider like it's the sheer amount of jammy toast that's forcing them open.

~ Anyway, I've made my mind up what we're going to do, and we can't start doing it until you're dressed and sorted, so get moving, I say with a tone of obvious impatience, and Danny nods and slurps at the milky tea and munches and slurps and nods again before wiping her big jammy moosh on the sleeve of her gown and heading off to prepare.

Of course, I'm lying to dearest Danny. I haven't a plan, and I don't know if she'll be the slightest bit interested in helping even if one comes to mind. But as she gets ready I stay put on the sofa for five minutes to gather myself, lay back, watch the silent silvery glint of jet pass high above our home, then with eyes shut and trying as hard as poss to let myself get calm and focussed, I can see a rough plan forming, and then I'm watching the big white condensation trail above slowly splitting and spreading into thinner, weaker threads with puffing whorly fringes when I remember Gerry's maudlin mood the previous evening and her mention of her man.

~ Who's Gerry going with again? I shout through to Danny, who turns down her music as I repeat the question.

She appears at the door, struggling to fasten the strap of her sports bra, and it is indeed a chest that requires considerable support. Her hair is all over the place and she looks a proper sight, but you can see the muscles move in her shoulders and side as she shifts to secure the catch, and I ponder her strength. Powerful lass, our Danny. I have to keep her closer than ever, despite any misgivings I may have about her overall attitude to Joanne. Things could get hairy and Danny is valuable.

~ What's-his-face, that wee guy, Josie, Josie Quinn.

~ Any idea where he lives? I ask then, and Danny thrusts her chest out and manually arranges her breasts within the sturdy cups.

~ Over in the old U-block, she says, as if I should have known.

The U-block? Oh dear. I get on the phone, rouse Kelly and Gerry from their sloth, and before the hour is out I've got my little ladies behind me and we're out again in the lovely fresh sunlit day, plodding with a definite spring towards the only part of the whole estate where no mail is ever delivered, rozz never drop by to say hello (regardless of whatever mayhem is happening), and the residents break down into four main categories – rats, cats, dogs, and humans, in decreasing numerical order.

Gerry is in rather sheepish mode, hanging behind slightly as we near the block, which is arranged like the shape of a U, hence the startling originality of the nickname, and I suppose she's getting a bit worried over what this is all about as I haven't really spoken to her and Kelly as such about what's afoot, and only Danny has the slightest notion of what urgency is driving me now.

Kelly is a bit hyper, all gibbering and over-the-top about some wildlife prog she watched about penguins, but she's always like that after a night on the Flash, especially if she's been smoking as well, and I suspect that she probably stayed up until the wee hours having a puffy session with Gerry.

Even with it being a rather cold day, the smell of the block is as sweaty and festery as usual, putting me in mind of the honk that comes across the hill from the brewery on the rare occasions when the Easterly wind is prevalent.

U-block is as ugly as ugly could ever be, the flat cement panels covered with dodgy early seventies squiggles and chunky geometric shapes which may have been the epitome of cutting edge architectural chic at the time, but now are naffably laughably awful and dark green streaked with moss and mushroom-type spreading growths, all drainpipes askew and small like trees and bushes growing from the guttering. The entire place was due for demolition many moons ago, but there was a scandalous scam which erupted into the papers and caused all manner of political shenanigans, and folk were bumped from top desk-jobs and there was talk of cash changing hands in brown envelopes, and even the rozz were getting up to their necks, so the whole demolition thing fell through among much pointing of fingers and general buck-passing.

At one time the U-block was being given awards, named as a shining example of new urban whatever, and there was indeed a good selection of shops and community-related facilities for folk to use, and when the shut-down came and all residents were tearfully packed off to other award winning schemes here, hither and yon, some of them decided not to go and organised a sit-in, all guitars and drunken nostalgia about the good old days. They too eventually got fed up with being covered in mushrooms and having rats crawling up their bog-pans and so fled, with the result being that the block became a magnet for needlers, underage riders and the boozing roofless by day and night alike. Josie had apparently moved in with a team of needling squatters on the top floor, though Gerry assured us that her man was not into breaking the blood-air barrier and was there as a protest against some unspecified injustice.

Not knowing exactly where to go, I beckon Gerry to the fore.

~ Right, Gerry dearest, this is your man's patch so

you can do the honourables, and dear Gerry shuffles forward rather gloomy and red-faced and altogether unhappy with the situation. She's been going with this lad for about three months or so since she met him in the pool hall one night, and very intense it seems too, but our Gerry is most quiet and private and shy when it comes to talking about him, and she will only ever divulge details of how daft she is about him, and he her, when she is out of her head, and even then she is guarded and prefers to dreamily moon and glaze rather than supply extensive details. So there's an element of girly curiosity about this visit which she probably dreads.

It gets noticeably dodgier as we walk cautious-style along the main corridor overlooking the central court of U-block which is a veritable jungle of plastic-bag bearing trees and wide brown puddles covered with rainbowy oil whorls and miscellaneous garbage everywhere. And the darkened doorways beneath the landings are well worth great wariness, with occasional shufflings and shifting of shapes betraying the movements of cats and rats and human brats, these latter deserving of particular respect, many being solvent-headed wannabees who will be about their business of robbing for older gangers or perhaps relatives housebound with needle cravings, so we string out single-file and take it very careful and wary, Gerry in front with me behind and Danny protecting the rear behind wee Kelly. I have a wee half-jump when a rather frantic shout comes from a flat as we pass, but Gerry strolls on indifferent, and it seems she feels quite relaxed hereabouts.

So we come to the door, already partly-opened, of a boarded-up flat, much graffitied with fluorescent green

P-Zone and MHK hieroglyphs, and older menshies saying RUCKO and FTQ and sundry other crudities which, to the initiated, provide many clues as to the turbulent history of this place.

Gerry bangs the steel door-cover three times rapid and a happy shout comes from some chap within.

~ Gerry-babe, in you come, says this male, and she sort of half-glances at me before moving a wee bit closer to the gap, all wary and white now.

~ Josie! she shouts, the happy male voice not, apparently, belonging to her amour, and there is much shuffling and coughing inside before a quieter voice, much nearer, pipes up.

~ Hi, Gerr, and out he comes, squinting and as wary and white as she.

I move beside Gerry and beckon him closer. He stays put. I extend my right hand.

~ Hi, Josie. Much heard of. I'm Suzy, and he takes my hand and holds it rather than shakes it, and it occurs to me that his chap is not entirely awake or straight, and perhaps has been telling porkies to Gerry regarding his drug intake.

~ Hope you don't mind us coming up with Gerry un-announced like this. We would've called first, but what with you not having a phone and that, you know.

It's a bit of a strain being nice to this character, especially as he kind of shifts back and to the side a tad, as if wanting whoever is inside to hear what I'm saying. And I can see now that he truly is a creature of slobboid type, all patchy blue bristle about the numerous chins, a complex jigsaw of food and drink slabber stains all over the layered t-shirts, an apparently solidified lumber-shirt tied about his spare tyre, greyish blue training pants with matching knee-holes, and massive hill-walking socks pulled up to his knees. He is the sorriest sight I have seen for a long time, and Gerry's obvious discomfiture suggests that this may well be the very first time she has had the opportunity to view her man in light of like natural type.

~ So what's up then? he asks Gerry, his crumbling dentoids showing tan and cream.

I feel a distinct urge to chuck, but a figure in the background, inside the flat, catches my attention. With no light inside the place, it's almost impossible to make out anything past the first ten feet or so of the narrow hallway, but then there's a mumble and a shrill chatter from a room within, and a human belching sound becomes a muffled curse and then there's an insane squawking accompanied by more loud cursing, then Josie flattens himself against the steel door and I jump almost out of my skin as three chickens come belting towards me, flapping horrible wee scrawny wings and their shiny eyes looking at me sidey-ways. I hop back, right onto Danny's foot, and she lets out a howl and collapses back against the landing barrier and the two of us end up on the deck and are prone and powerless when the doorway fills up with the biggest guy I have ever seen in my life.

The chickens appear to have tasted freedom before, and know which way they want to go, and this great lumbering giant obviously knows it too, and he does the human equivalent of a hand-brake turn in order to control the vastness of his frame, skidding to a halt just inches from my feet, then takes off down the walkway in pursuit of the still grobbling and clawking things, a trail of hovering feathers in their path.

~ Babies! shouts the giant as they all descend the stairwell at the end of the walkway, and I get back to my feet, Danny also rising, grimacing like mad and clutching at her ankle.

Kelly is laughing, and making no effort whatever to disguise her amusement, despite my obvious embarrassment. I feel myself flush a tad, and get a sudden urge to speed things up somewhat, this giant's appearance having disconcerted me more than a little.

~ Josie, I say, and he turns to me, looking slightly more awake now, but still ultra-wary.

~ What do you know about the knifing up at Magenta Wednesday night?

He looks over at Gerry with a sort of pleading glance, as if hoping that she might be able to blast the correct answer to him by way of some extra-sensory perception type ray-beam.

~ What makes you think I know anything about it? he asks then, and with a note of shaky bravado that angers me, so I step nearer and I can feel my eyeballs widen and my cheeks drain.

Gerry groans, and pointedly turns her face away, and he knows he's in shit-street and starts waving his palms about a bit, the brave façade cracked and gone before it was ever really up.

~ Right, right, I know Gerry must have told you already. Right, right. No bother, right. No bother. It's cool. No bother, and as he says all this it's as if he's talking to himself and not me.

He scans about a bit, then steps back and makes a very gushy and gentlemanly gesture indicating an invitation to enter, which we do.

With all windows steel-boarded, the darkness is

thick, but the flat, which is surprisingly large, is not as grotty as might be expected. A small lamp in what must be the living room is dimmed to soft redness by a silk-type scarf partly draped over it, and the effect is rather brothelous, but gives enough light for us to see where we are. Josie bids us sit, which Gerry and Kelly do, but wearing my white Palmer jeans and still thinking about those chickens, I decline and stay standing as Josie quickly passes a leather pouch to Gerry and then squats cross-legged and starts building the skins.

~ I didn't see it all, well, I saw it all but I couldn't see it that well from up on the bridge.

~ What bridge? I ask, and I'm trying to picture it all as he speaks.

~ Brewery-path. I was just back from the town, got off the sixty-three, walked over.

~ Brave lad you, Danny says, and I'm mildly annoyed at her interruption but in fairness she's just voiced exactly what I was thinking.

Josie laughs.

~ Naw, that's just 'cos I fell asleep on the bus, missed the stop.

This modest and honest style causes a ripple of mirth which endears him to all present, and Gerry moves across to lend the support which seems badly needed, poor Josie's hands trembling so much that he makes a pig's ear of the joint-wrap and crushes it into a tiny ball.

~ So I was like jogging you know, and then I see them down by Cerulean and I'm a bit like that, oh-ho, so I kind of hang back. There's Shuggs and a couple of his boys, Jimbo and him with the sideys, Jerso. They've their backs to me, giving it big arms and shouting down to the Maggie. So not having the specs on I can't really make out faces and such, but there's a team of six down at the Maggie car park, and they're sort of huddled, one standing out, and that's Joanne.

~ You just said you couldn't make them out, I say.

~ Right, I didn't know then it was her. But it was, and the others are sort of arms crossed and one of them pointing and such, and Shuggs and his boys are sort of heading down, still shouting like ho, what's up and all that, but it's like this squad's just ignoring them, like they're looking up glances but more bothered about what's happening right there, and Shuggs and the two Jays start running down, and two of this squad move away from their mates and go into their jackets and whatever it is they take out, Shuggs slams the brakes on and turns and gives it heavy sprint back to his own patch.

~ Guns? I ask, and he shakes his head.

~ I don't know. Might've been. Can't imagine Shuggs running like that if it was just a standard flicker what with him always having his own anyway.

Josie speaks sense.

~ So Shuggs and his boys are back at the edge of the Cherry car-park, just by the recycling bins, and they kind of hang about. Then the wee group down the Maggie suddenly moves back and away from the front door, as if they're heading back to the Spring path, and this one suddenly goes for Joanne, punches her a couple of times, and then they walk away. Joanne's on her back when they walk off, she sits up, goes back down again half on her front, starts crawling. The wee group stops just at the entrance to the bins, and one runs back and hits her head a couple of times, drags her about six, maybe eight feet, and leaves her sort of slumped at the big light support at the car park corner. They go out of sight for a wee minute 'cos I can't see the whole car park from there, then this four-drive comes out slow, doesn't use the entrance, it goes right over the grass, you know by the wee swing-park, then along the Spring path and goes back onto the slip just before the carriageway signs.

~ Many other bodies about the Cherry basket or Magenta when this happened? I ask, and he shakes his head.

~ Like I say, Shuggs and the Jays probably saw as much as me, must've had a better view of faces and what-not being closer and that, but I can't say it was busy. This is tea-time mind, everyone's in. There's a few faces at windows, especially down at the Maggie cos they can like hear what's going on, but no, there wasn't many folk about at all.

~ So what did you do then? Danny asks, and again her intervention nicks me but in a way it's good that she's showing an interest.

~ I went back, he says, looking down.

~ You went back over the brewery-path? I ask, and the incredulity in my voice sparks renewed wariness in him, and he looks up wide-eyed and defensive.

~ We get plenty of shit as it is from the rozz, Suzy, you know how it is. Imagine the rozz turning up and I just happen to be passing by the Maggie and someone's just been done in? They'd have me down the Spring in jig-time. I went back over to the hospital bridge, then cut over the cemetery and came in the back, across the motorway.

I sit down on the ancient sofa, forgetting the whiteness of my breeks and not caring any more about anything. No further on.

~ Josie, I believe what you're telling me. Problem is, see, I was down Spring station this morning, and those boys have got me down for this I reckon. Could you see enough to say for sure it wasn't me? I say very normal and almost quietish, as if I'm just thinking out loud.

Josie looks me long in the eye before cupping a hand over Gerry's and shaking his head.

~ Honest truth. If the rozz come seeking eye-dee from me, I can't tell them a thing, and it's a scoosh for them to prove I can barely make out figures let alone faces at that distance. I know it wasn't you 'cos I've seen you about a lot, I know the way you walk, I can tell all you girls from a distance. These people were not Maggies or Cherries, and certainly not from U-block. That much I can say for sure, but if the cops push me to say aye or nay to a face, I'm up a gum tree and no mistake. I'm sorry Suzy. You know what I mean?

I nod wearily, knowing full well that Gerry's man, slobboid and crumbling youngster though he may be, is no thicko, and has pretty well anticipated the likely course of events should he be pressed for a statement.

~ There's one other thing, he says then.

He pauses, as if filling up, maybe ready to gush. Gerry puts an arm about his back and kind of pulls him towards her the once in an admittedly touching gesture, and he kind of half-smiles at her before facing me again.

~ Shuggs and his boys went down after the four-drive was offsky.

A spark now and I lean forward, eager.

~ They went down very slow like, I suppose they were expecting rozz, but they must've been curious.

~ And what happened? I say, and I'm getting anxious and a tad hyper.

~ They sort of went up behind her, and they stopped like they didn't want to go any nearer, but eventually Shuggs sort of walks in a big circle round to face her, and he's got the hands in the pockets and all that and he's looking about pure panicky, then he goes right up to her, and kind of crouches, and he doesn't touch her, but it's as if he's talking to her, maybe a minute or something like that, and the two Jays come up as well, but they sort of hang back and one of them is getting really jumpy you know, walking away and walking back and I can catch sort of half-shouts from him, like he's wanting to split. Then the siren starts up, the usual, coming from over the Spring, and the two Jays take off, and Shuggs just hangs on a split second longer but then he's off as well.

Right. That's enough. I stand up, ready to thank young Josie and be on my way with my little ladies when there is another ruckus and the outer door bangs and the inner door opens and the three chickens come in, only slightly less distressed than on the last occasion we met. And when the door is fully opened and the chicken-catcher enters, he has to bow his head slightly to get through the standard six-four doorframe.

He crosses the room with four or five strides, ignoring all present, and peeks through the slightly ajar door in the corner by the boarded window. This, presumably, is where the chickens live, and he stares into the unseen space for a few seconds, muttering, then gently closes the door over and turns to us with an expression that can best be described as curious. Josie does the honours.

~ Maxo, this is Suzy. You know, Gerry's boss, he says, and I get a slight twingle at the use of the word, technically accurate though it may be.

The monster moves to the centre of the room, and very slowly scans Danny and Kelly as Gerry points them out. Then he turns to face me, and all the years of being told that size is meaningless suddenly seem to count for nothing. He must be six-six or seven, lean of waist and limb, but massively shouldered, the old sweatshirt appearing to contain pads of some kind. His face is lightly bearded and filthy, but there is a smoothness about his skin and a symmetry of his features which is strikingly attractive to me, and I get the sort of tummy-tingle I haven't felt since I used to daydream about Peter Cranston back in the wee school days. He smiles, and it's alarming to find that the lower front four choppers are missing, but the smile is genuine enough and he extends a hand which could cover my face with inches to spare on all sides.

~ John. John Doohihan. My pals call me Maxo, so you can if you want, he says so friendly and genuine that I smile like a wee star-struck teeny-screamer and am speechless what with being sort of awed.

Then his smile disappears and he frowns.

~ I apologise. I didn't, I mean, I'm sorry about your friend. Gerry and Josie were telling me. Terrible. Really terrible, he says, and I'm busy trying to place the guy's accent as I stutter out a reply.

~ Yeah, it's terrible. We're trying to find out what it's all about, but Josie's given me a bit of a lead so we'll really have to be getting off. I'd love to stay and chat but -

My little ladies get up then, well, Kelly and Danny

do. Gerry stays camped on the bare floorboards beside her dearest Josie.

~ It's nice meeting you, John. Sorry if we disturbed your, your hens? I say, not at all sure what these beasts should best be described as.

~ No problem, he smiles. The little cluckers are out every chance they get. Does them good to get chased about once in a while. Does me no harm either.

~ Suzy?

It's Josie. Gerry is still sort of half-holding him, but he looks very shaky, almost ill and she's staring at him and very concerned-looking, and he's looking at me, all sort of half-filled up and very weak of voice.

~ Suzy, you must know you've got a bit of a rep round here now. You always did, right enough, but since you started with that job there's a lot of growling in the Cherry basket and elsewhere when it comes to it. There's folk will be glad to place you there, maybe even say it was you. I know it wasn't you, and I'll tell them so no problem. I know we don't have much clout about here. Folk would rather just pretend we don't exist period. But if you need back-up, we're behind you. Crash any time you like.

I nod my appreciation and make for the door, but a last question springs up and I pause in the doorway as Gerry rises to her feet and helps Josie to his.

~ Maxo, or John, sorry, I, well, I don't mean to be nosey or that, but I'm surprised I haven't seen you about before, you know, what with—

And speechless again, I sort of just raise my eyebrows and he laughs.

~ Yeah, I know what you mean. I'm not exactly un-obtrusive. Let's just say I'm very shy.

I smile and nod and leave, Danny and Kelly behind, and we take our time going back down the landing, allowing Gerry some time with her man. Danny and Kelly chatter excitedly about how gorgeous Maxo is as I ponder how to go about what has to be the next step. Shuggs will be on red alert if he sees us anywhere near the Cherry basket, but there's no option but to talk to him now. If she managed to say anything to him, it could be the breakthrough I'm after. I know if I call he'll just take it auto-tape, and even if I try to arrange a meet he'll fear a trap, and rightly so, for until Gramps cleared him I would certainly have laid money on Shuggs being cold of nose and hard of toes by the week's end, but Shuggs doesn't know I've seen Gramps.

But now the whole thing has flipped and I must try to talk with the guy who attempted to sever my spinal column. It does not cross my mind to question whether or not this is all worth it, well not right then it doesn't. And I can be truthful in saying that it is more than self-interest which motivates me now.

Fact – Joanne was murdered by unknown tickets, almost certainly not locals. Fact – it wasn't Shuggs and his merry Cherroids. Fact – some wild and scary Southside team is after me and my little ladies, and we know not why. Fact – the rozzloiderlings are taking my measurements and the Commissioner's Office is going to considerable bother and expense to keep them away from me. It all swirls and spins and makes like a jigsaw of nonsense in my head, and so many people and so many facts, but so little reason or meaning. Something big and snarly and nasty is going on and we're all stuck in it now whether we like it or not, and even if Joanne wasn't the friend she was, even if we had never clapped eyes on each other, events have crowded about so hard and fast that we are all caught inside them.

Gerry catches up with us as we reach the top of the main road leading from U-block back to civilisation as most know it, and is red-eyed and sniffy. Kelly gives her one of her cleaner snot-rags and Gerry parps sporadically into it as we plod up towards the junction.

Where to now? The Hall beckons, protective and with promise of Flash and hash and whatever other pain-numbing pleasures we may care to choose, so we drift towards the crossroads at the roundabout in silence, but probably pondering pretty much the same heaviness.

We turn at the junction and maintain a steady plod, the sun shining down on our backs, sniffing in the cold air and watching, always watching, as we pass The Depot and the pee-oh and the freezer shop, and for everyone else it appears to be just another day of shopping and queuing and gossiping and boozing and sleeping and schooling and work.

Here a body nods and smiles, there at the corner a pair of young guys turn and flee, juking up a close in the old tenement block which runs along the hill behind the pool hall. The mid-afternoon bingo session has just finished and there's like two thousand old dears streaming out of the big doors onto the special old dear buses that take them back to their blocks or schemes or wherever else they bide, and shiny black taxis are taking away the ones who maybe won or maybe think themselves above taking the old dear special, and then we're down the hill by the old mill wall, past the bookies and the video shop and the offy, and there's a bit of shouting going on in The Cross Arms, which is like a prehistoric pub at that corner, so we speed up a tad lest we get embroiled in some mid-day drinking brawl, and then the hall is in sight and we slow a tad and enjoy a last few minutes of bright Autumn sun before entering the windowless building.

I remember that half-hour walk very clearly now, and it still is sharp and bright, and maybe I half-realised it at the time and that's why my mind grabbed such a tight hold of it, but it was to be the very last time that me and my little ladies walked in daylight as a team without hassle and worry, with some kind of place in the area, some kind of clout. We were worth attention then, indeed, we were watched very carefully by some. But after that night, nothing would ever be the same, cos one of us was soon to be cold of nose and hard of toes, that is to say, yeah, dead.

CHAPTER EIGHT

Grass-creeping four-drives, giants with chickens as pets, grumpy high-flyer lawyers, frowning scheming silk-tied rozz, scar-faced bitches from the far-flung South and everywhere fingers, fat pointing fingers, and all pointing squarely at me.

The Hall is completely empty when we traipse in, fresh of face and slightly puffed what with the briskness of the walk and the sharp coldness of the afternoon, the sun already dropping low and blazing red above the hospital chimney.

Thanks to the clocks dropping back overnight it's suddenly shifted into official Winteriness, and those who suffer from the sunlight deprivation and associated depressive disorders (such as Mum) will be mooching about, glumness incarnate, and those of a superstitious bent (such as Danny) are whispering dire warnings about Friday's full moon being highly significant and worthy of some dread.

Seated at our table, I lay all known details out for the

consideration of my little ladies. They listen close and sip quietly at the Flash shandies, professional strictness decreeing that any serious quaffing will have to wait until the business in hand has been resolved.

And the business, as I propose it, meets with general approval. I want my little ladies to know that they are under no obligation to help. It is myself who faces the soapy bubble, that much is clear, and so I figure it wisest and fairest to allow the departure of one or all at this juncture, but it is heart-gladdening to find that, if anything, the ladies are offended by the suggestion, and urge me to talk no more on it. Instead, they assure me of their loyalty and shared enthusiasm to find Joanne's killer, then set up a table and enjoy a leisurely knock-about while I get on the blower and make the calls we've agreed.

Declan the manager is fine about it all, and offers me the use of the private lounge, this being a snooker room with telly-room attached which has space for up to fifteen bodies, so is ideal, especially as he will charge only for drinks and any titbits consumed. We fix the time at seven, thus allowing for those I seek to finish whatever jobs they may have, do tea with families, shower etc. Giving such little notice, as I am, I have to make sure the individuals do not feel they are being taken advantage of, and so I agree with Declan that he will accept no cash from any involved, and also promise to owe him three-ton to secure the booking and cover the first few rounds as well as payment for the two door-stoppers Declan wants to have there just in case.

Clearing the air with my little ladies seems to help no end, and I realise the prospect of having problems with them must have been troubling me a lot more than I realised. Now that I know they're sticking by me and with me and behind me, everything seems much clearer. In our time together so far, I've always kept the ladies very much at arm's length. That's management skills I suppose. Being nice, but still not a chum to any, even cousin Danny. And although I know that they probably know that and take it into account when assessing their relationship with me, I've always kept enough distance so that there's an element of wondering there – none is good enough to take me on single-handed, but they could as a team. The tetatet with Danny was the chance for Kelly or Gerry to nail mutinous colours if they were so minded, but apart from the mild support of Kelly, Danny lost out good and proper and has kept her gob pretty well shut since. This support from them now is a relief and a vote of confidence, and is certainly over and above the call of the proverbial as far as standard LO duties are concerned.

So we all know what we have to do, and there's time enough for a quick half-Flash and just the teeniest toot of a moderately loaded joint before I take my leave, Danny with me, and we jump a fast-black hack into the town. I could easily use the bank in the Spring but I don't want to run the risk of bumping into anyone who might cause distractions.

Danny is more serious and alert than I've ever seen her, her eyes flashing hither and yon at great speed on the edgy for anything or anyone dodgy, and she actually walks just a half-pace behind me, as if she's literally watching my back, and that pleases me no end given that just twenty-four hours before I was slapping her ears and threatening to puncture her eyeballs with my shiny nails. But as we pace down the Bucky towards the bank, drawing glances of admiration and dread what with our black-and-whiteness and steel-toedness, it occurs that it is quite obviously in Danny's interest now to watch my back. After all, the set-up is mine. I'm the boss, and if I come to a sticky end then so does her income. I know that Danny knows that I know quite as well as her that she would not be able to run the team – the practical side of things is no problem at all, and she is quite as capable as me of persuading someone to part with cally. But her problem with letters and numbers means that the paperwork would do for her, and relying on someone else to do that side of things leaves you wide open to rip-offs.

The bank people are very off-hand and gloopy-mouthed when I go in, Danny in tow, and request an immediate meet with the Miss Burgess who was most obliging and accessible when I opened my account and lodged my first wage and share of takings. Not so accessible and obliging now it seems, but I make sure the young man understands that I will not be leaving until I've spoken to her and withdrawn the amount I require, which is four thousand.

After twenty minutes of being ignored and watched very carefully by a kindly-faced security guard, Miss Burgess emerges and moves across the carpet towards us like a wee Japanese woman, tiny steps and a smile you couldn't crack with a sledgehammer. She listens to my request, all the while nodding, and continues to nod as she tells me it's out of the question, then I tell her that my account will be closed and I show her the card of Miss Warnes the CO's lawyer, and tell her that my friend Miss Warnes will personally see to it that the entire Commissioner's Office account is shifted to the first competing bank which springs to mind, whereupon she continues nodding, smile intact all the while, and walks backwards into someone's office, coming back out three minutes later with a stamped release which I swap at the counter for four slidey shiny plastic sealed bags containing spilt-new steel-ribboned twenties.

Only four hours till the meeting, so we shift hot-foot to a salon of Danny's choosing called Number Six, and we both get taken right away. I get the blonde-streaky mess well and truly sorted thanks to the application of an intense black colourant which gleams turquoise-blue when dry, and now that it's freed from the trusty band I'm surprised at how long it is. I explain to the lad that I'm going somewhere I'd rather not be recognised, that I'm after a totally new look, and when he shows me how to alter the appearance of my facial features with some very dense and rather greasy-feeling foundation which is, apparently, the favoured brand of professional theatrical artistes and photo-shoot models, the transformation wouldn't be out of place in one of those before-and-after lifestyle rags.

Danny is delighted with her cut, which hasn't taken much off the medium length, but given it a swirly and quite dry officey style which makes her look much older and quite sane.

Then it's back up Bucky to Frazzini's and Gerome's and Jazz Break for slack casuals, the tippermost of cutting-edge chic but mostly unlabelled, which is more important than anything else, and then to Polly Tranter's, where I find the kind of ankle-supporting soft-bottomed boots I've been looking out for of late but never seen anywhere bar heavyweight dress-style mags. Danny fancies a pair of high-heeled suede Steelos but they will have to wait for another time, impractical as they are.

Another hour and a half has zipped away. Into Rammer, which is maybe the dearest label shop in the whole of the centre, but we know Sally-Anne, who was at school with Danny and is manageress, and she gives us a scan at the stock which has been slightly soiled or returned or found wanting in whatever other way, and all labels have been removed, so we select enough tops, jackets and accessories to cover Kelly and Gerry, and Sally-Anne is most delighted when I press five fresh twenties into her hand instead of the meagre fifty she shakily requested, and is happy to understand that we never were in the store and she never saw us, even if anyone else did.

Danny, with half a dozen carrier bags hanging on each arm, squeezes herself into a cab and heads off back to the Hall to dump the gear and make sure Kelly and Gerry have completed the errand assigned them. I get the very next hack and politely request that he wait for me outside Henry's Arcade as I quickly scour the second-hand jewellery stalls for something for Mum. Maybe it's just some kind of wishful thinking, but every time she calls saying that she's coming to visit I rush out and get her a wee trinket in the hope that this will somehow guarantee an appearance. There's a small hardwood box under my bed that must have about a dozen items of reasonably expensive Deco bracelets, rings, and a stoater of a necklace made of amber lumps joined with silver loops. It's her birthday next week, so maybe she will turn up right enough. If not, the plan is that I'll go visit at Christmas whether I'm invited or not, and give her the whole lot like some high-class lucky bag. I find a lovely wee solid silver double-heart locket with tiny sparkly stones glinting every known colour afront and knock the guy down from a ton to seventy-five. When I get back out the cabbie has moved to the other side of the road and is having a heated discussion with a gloopy-faced wasp, but I calm him down with the twenty-five I saved on the locket and urge him to get me to Viewhill as swiftly as he is able.

But swift as I am sure the rather good-looking young man would like to be, the traffic on the carriageway to Viewhill is as jam-packed as can be, and we grumble along in the fast lane at little more than walking pace for almost half an hour. Even with the glass shutter closed over I can hear him cursing everyone and everything, and every now and then he checks me out in his wee mirror and I can feel his eyes scanning as much of me as can be scanned in a rather drooly fashion which is fairly repulsive but makes me feel that the new look was perhaps worth it.

Having totally reinvented myself in the space of three hours, I'm pretty sure I can get in and out of Magenta unnoticed, but this theory collapses when Kieran the Door emerges from his box-house as soon as I get through the main sliders.

~ Suzy, he says, his wrinkly concern writ large, the rozz have been in again, you've just missed them, fifteen minutes tops.

~ Any names, I ask, and he shakes vigorously and places a hand on my arm as if preparing me for bad news.

~ Suzy, listen doll, I've had about ten calls asking for

you, folk trying to get your number and all that, a couple of them right bad ones, real heavy stuff by the way, threats and what-not. You shouldn't be here doll, you know.

I flick all available fingers towards myself.

~ What do you think all this is about then?

~ Aye, well, I was going to say there, you look great by the way, so you do.

~ I'm not into looking great, Kieran, I'm into looking like someone else, anyone else bar me.

~ Suzy, he says, his hand still grasping my forearm, tell me it wasn't you.

I say nothing, but look at him pure and hard, and he lowers his eyes and nods and releases my arm and beckons me to follow him to his box. Inside, he grabs a padded envelope from a high shelf and slips it into the big Gerome bag.

~ I need it back, as soon as you can manage.

I slip my free hand into the bag and squeeze the thick packet.

~ The rozz already took the master tapes for that night, but this is the house copy that covers what happened. There's not a lot on it. I've already checked. But you might get something off it. Please, Suzy, please make sure you get it back to me or I'm in serious, serious shit.

I feel a sudden urge to gush copiously, and grab him about the neck and draw him near and plant a kiss which I target for his forehead but he moves his face up, as males do, and it ends up squashing the end of his long, vein-busted nose.

~ You're a pure gem, Kieran. You'll get it back, I say, and then I'm off and up in the box, mind abuzz with a million things to do, then slip the yale in, door opens, and

I freeze, stomach cramps when I realise that the mortice wasn't locked and the telly-room lights are on and someone is in my house, and it can't be one of my little ladies.

Someone is in my house.

Fear is a complicated thing, I think. Way back in the first year, when I was going to karate at the Nex, Miss Wilko used to make sure that I was there for the open evenings and stuff, the nights when the club was maybe having a friendly with another school, or else showing the parents what sort of stuff we were up to. She always put me out against folk who were much bigger than me, height-wise, weight-wise, and usually both, and she did it to demonstrate that size isn't a big deal, that it's attitude and speed and skill and all that that really counts. I knew what she was doing because she explained very clearly to me that she really felt I had the right attitude, that I had no fear. I didn't know what she meant.

Maybe it's just that everyone gets scared by different things, just like everyone seems to get turned on by different things. I don't really know. But I know for sure that I've never been scared by people, by muscles or scary faces or darkness or screeching violins, the usual stuff. If you ask me, people get scared of things because they think they should be scared by them, because they want to do the right thing, and the right thing is to be frightened. I can't think that way.

What scares me is my imagination. If I can see what I'm up against, I can rattle through the available options, decide what's best, then go ahead and see what happens. If I end up with a crinkly mouth and bruised extremities, fair enough – I know next time to choose a different option.

Even darkness can be overcome with sense and patience. We trained for three months solid in my last club, doing moves in darkness, our sensei bringing us closer together week by week, so that eventually we were having sparring sessions in pitch blackness, and if anything we probably had fewer minor injuries than usual, even though the sessions were just as tough. I learned to listen, to smell, to develop my sense of touch to the extent where I could map body heat like one of those multi-coloured aerial photos of cities or fleeing criminals or whatever, and I swear I could hear air moving – not limbs and cloth, but the air they move in, I could hear the air itself pulse and shape about anything moving within it. That was in the new dojo down by the casino where the sensei is this like living legend character who can knock people over by looking at them, and there I was used pretty much as a punch bag by a lot of older students, mostly men, who were perhaps not quite as intensely into the karate ethos as they would have had the teacher believe and were not above having a sly rub at my female parts when clinches were on, but this sleakit behaviour switched on my anger better than any pep talk or warm-up. So between the school club, then the Riverside club, plus all the training I did myself, I did my time long and slow and took many knocks on the way but it all served to confirm what Miss Wilko had always maintained – that I fear no-one.

It's only when I know an enemy is there but can bring no sense to focus upon it that I feel fear, and perhaps more intensely than most, because if I feel it then I know I am in trouble, and to know that you are in trouble means panic, and panic is more dangerous than fear because panic means a loss of control.

*

And I feel it now, standing in the open doorway of my own flat, with over five tons worth of gear hanging in bags on my arm, and a jangly set of keys in the other. I am in trouble, and the realisation of it almost makes me wet myself.

Rozz? A private sent by someone? Kieran knows someone came up and didn't say? Disgruntled locals in lynch-mode?

Every nerve and cell of me is saying that I've walked into a set-up, and I should turn about right now and flee.

But I can't. This is my house, my home, whether I like it or not, and I've done nothing wrong that I should run away from it. The anger builds, but I check my wee mercury level, and mentally calm the surface to purely polished flatness. If they're still here, I will kill them, rozz or otherwise.

I take one step across to the toilet door, careful to put my weight on the only part of the carpet where I know there will be no creaking of board beneath, place the bags within the door, carefully curl the keys into my palm and make the fist solid.

There is after-shave in the air, so slight a waft it could perhaps be from myself via the cab, or the new clothes, but it is definitely there, masculine and slightly sweet. And another smell, familiar, but muted and distant.

Three quick silent steps to the telly-room door, and the bastard is shut. Since I got the new carpet in, the door makes a soft but audible scraping when opened, so whoever is inside will certainly be alerted, if they haven't already noted the yale going in.

Scanning about weapons-wise, nothing handy in the hall, but I know that inside the telly-room, just slotted in beside the display cabinet, there should be a two-foot hollow barbell pole.

A voice comes, male and low, not whispering, but quietish, and I guess he's at the far end of the room, near the windows, perhaps at the door of the kitchenette. The other or others may be in the kitchen then, so it's as good a time as any.

I push the door open with my left, and half an eye to quickly confirm the tool is there, crouch and lean and grab it, the guy is over by the windows right enough and he's big, but slow moving back when he sees me and opens his mouth to shout but hands raise, no weapon, and I've the bar at waist height and three paces over and I'm about to bring it up across his neck when another figure moves into the kitchenette doorway and just as well she screams otherwise I would hit him first and then turn to her.

~ Francine!

In the space of like half a minute I've dropped the bar and we're cuddling each other and all the stuff about Joanne starts flooding out and I'm gushing like a new born babe and she moves me to the sofa where I gush on in truly pathetic mode as the male who came so close to a severe tanking stays in the kitchenette making tea.

She looks well, very smart and smiley, and her man is called Guy and he's a train driver and has two girls my age and it all sounds pretty hunky-dory. He's understandably quiet what with just having been threatened, but I apologise profusely and he's all nods and weak smiles.

Mum is annoying me what with kind of perching herself ever so lady-like on the edge of the sofa and making sure she puts her mug back on the coaster in between sips, all the more to impress this bloke who stays silent and white as she frowns and leans forward and grabs my hand and cups it and looks deep into my eyes with what I suppose she imagines to be maternal concern.

~ Francine, this job you're doing, it's been in the papers you know. They're not doing it down our way, not yet anyway, but they're thinking of starting it and it's an awful mess, just last week, wasn't it Guy, more demonstrations about it, big ones too. It's awful dangerous dear. Don't you think you're just a bit on the young side for this type of thing? she asks, and this reference to danger sets alarm bells a-ring as I don't recall ever telling her that I was a Liaison Officer as such, only that I was working for the Commissioner's Office on data processing.

Perhaps Mum is more sussed than I've ever given her credit for, and I do have to concede that she looks genuinely worried.

~ Listen, Mum, I say as I take back my hand and get up, I'll get on with my job and you get on with yours. I'm a big girl now and you're really not doing me any favours worrying about me. In fact, you're just making things worse.

~ Your mother's very concerned, pipes up this male, and I turn my head very slowly to where he's got his arse parked in my telly chair.

I have to be careful. Mum has a rather sparky temper on her at times, and although she's never been remotely interested in training or formal combat of any kind, I'm not so big that she won't slap my ear and she knows I know it.

~ Sorry, I say to this guy Guy, but I don't really think this is any of your business.

~ You're upsetting your mother, and Sylvia's business is my business now, and this comes from him so straight and rather too cool for my liking, so I step aside the coffee table and smile as I look him up and down.

~ What do you mean by that? I say, and he looks at Mum, who looks at him and knows I'm looking at her but she doesn't look up at me as she puts the mug down again and makes a basket with her fingers.

~ Guy and me, we've decided, well, we're going to get married. Well, I should say, we're going to get engaged. Actually, we are engaged, we just have to get a ring. We wanted you to be the first to know, dear.

And it's only then that she looks up at me, and I feel such a wave of revulsion and surprise and just general shock and amazement that I can do nothing bar look at her, then look at him, then look at her again with what I suppose must be total like disgust.

~ Well you could say something, she says as I reach the door and I turn and pause, and I see her eyes full.

~ Congratulations, I mutter, and walk out, head a-spin.

Showering, most careful to avoid ruining the new hair and make-up job, I feel tender and soft, and reflect that the work-outs have been few and far between of late and sagginess of muscle is the result. It's impossible to run a finger along the full length of the scar Shuggs caused, but I always notice it, the knotty lumps, the ridge. I can't see him turning up, but if he doesn't, we may be able to organise a visit to his place. Danny should by now have started getting things organised in the Hall, and Gerry and Kelly will no doubt be ahop with excitement at the new wardrobe.

This nonsense with Mum could not have come at a worse time. Bad enough that she turns up in the midst of a crisis, but worse that she should create another with news of getting hitched to this character, who I'll bet she knows next to nothing about. That's the way Mum goes. Since she split with Dad she's been engaged four times. So this is the fifth in eleven years. I suppose that's maybe why she hasn't visited in so long, almost eight months. She dreads introducing me to these chaps as she knows full well I'll make little effort to know them or like them, and this one doesn't, going by first impressions anyway, seem to have anything outstand-ingly attractive about him that is likely to alter my established mode of behaviour.

By the time I'm changed into the new gear and get the make-up fixed again, I'm seriously running short of time. They're sat afront the box when I go back in, him with an arm uncomfortably high about the back of her head and her with eyes red and blurry mascara. I ask if they've eaten and she says no, so I suggest they call down for some boxes and I'll get it on my tab, but she's already ordered a Ruby for them, and me also, and much gloominess of face is the response when I say I can't stay much as I'd like to, that I'm late and must be for the off.

Quickly check the terminal. Five messages in. One from Mum, calling from the station to say she's on her way in a cab, the next is a two-second silence with background traffic noise. One from a client who we visited last week but were unable to contact due to presence of large dogs, sort of begging for one extra week. And then the last two messages are silences, one outdoors, the last sounding very pub-like and jazzy, much hubbub of young voices. Do the call-back but the number is not listed and unavailable publicly. There's also a whole massive stack of E-messages but I only ever get them from the CO's admin department and it's always dry-as-dust bumph like target projections and performance pie charts and such, so it can wait.

I get back into some tea and toast Mum's made me, and I know she's worried, but there's really no way I can hang on any longer. I look this guy, Guy, straight in the eye, and there is much wariness there, but he's likely still a bit wobbly.

~ Look, I'm sorry I can't stay, but it's not personal, and I'm sorry I'm a bit frantic. There's a lot on right now, and I wasn't expecting you. Congratulations on the engagement. I'm chuffed for you both. Here.

I give her the locket, still wrapped in the shop-paper, and her face lights up and he kind of bumshuffles forward in his seat as she opens it and sort of gasps, eyes wide, and she's giggling and sniffling and bubbling as she lifts it and gets him to fasten it for her. It looks good against her black blouse, tingly colours sparkling.

~ How did you? It's gorgeous, Francine, really, it's –

She starts bubbling heavy style, and he kind of pats and rubs her back and smiles up at me most patronisingly and I muster a smile in return which must surely be a grimace and I zip up my new black jerkin and make a point of jangling my keys in my pocket, eager now to get out.

~ When will you be back? she asks then.

~ Don't wait up, I say. I lean down to give her a kiss, and there's a moment of mad awkwardness when I wonder whether or not I should give him one as well, but think better of it and make a swift exit then, with a bag full of spare gear and various essentials.

Waiting for the box on its grinding cranking ascent, I feel the building sway as if for the first time, and get just a snatch of how panic-inducing and nauseating it was when we first moved in here, when I was only, what, six? I can remember Mum holding me as we both sat at the window that first winter evening, and we watched the lights and the clouds and the moonlit river heading off to the sea, and we both cried and the swaying was somehow Dad's fault, and Mum was sick and so was I and we were both up all night, cuddling on the sofa and taking turns to cry and comfort, and by daybreak it must've sunk in that this swaying cloud-bound place was our new house, and Dad wouldn't be coming back again, ever.

But now, as I give Kieran a discreet nod and head out into the windy night, already dark, the feeling, low and sickly but undeniable, is that I will not be coming back here. Whether or not the plan works out, my days in Viewhill have come to an end, and my eyelids brim with nippy saltiness and I pull my beret down a little and bow my head into the cold hard breeze and listen out for the tell-tale throb of diesel-driven cab.

CHAPTER NINE

Kelly greets me at the door of The Hall, and she looks fantastic, bright-eyed and the very height of cutting-edge chic, her hair tied back smartish with a black band, and smiling broad and full of zest as I've not seen her before. It's strange how sometimes when someone changes clothes or make-up or hair-style or whatever, you see them like it's for the first time and get an idea of what they're like afresh, and I find myself wondering how a lass as beautiful as her could have ended up doing this, being with me, with us, how she can be just one of my little ladies and not be on a catwalk or in movies or a teeny-band or whatever.

The boys on the door are, as I expected, Declan's nephews, Dave and Quasi, both top chaps and very civil, but skilled in a variety of combat arts and not to be lightly trifled with. I'm glad that they're on, although I very much doubt that they'd be able to stop any nastiness should it arise. Get involved, maybe, but stop it, no.

~ Jesus, Suzy, what's happening? Kelly asks, like she's on some new pill, but her eyes are clear and voice steady. I give her a reassuring arm-squeeze, but reveal nothing.

I sign myself in as normal (as Suzy Friel) and Kelly takes me to where my little ladies have already filled some bowls with peanuts and crisps of various flavourings. Then I notice a long low table at the back wall of the lounge, and Kelly's at my side as I get to it and lift up the corner of the massive napkin, which is like a gigantic piece of bog-roll lying atop all this grub. There's sausage rolls and pies and a big bowl of tossed salad and like pasta concoctions, and all mighty tasty-smelling and looking it is too, but I get a bit sort of freaked by this, and turn to Danny, who is busy trying to open a packet of breadsticks with her teeth. I'm ready to sound off about this being a meeting, not a fucking birthday party, when the swing doors open and Granda Pinks strides in with brother Jack, sons Harry, Jacko and Bobby, and nephews Gerrso, Hammy and Liam. The men advance immediately to the bar and salutations are shouted about while Gramps comes to me, unbuttons his best suit jacket and shakes hands before guiding me to the corner of the buffet table and peeking under the cover.

~ Nice spread, Suzy. I would've brought more of the boys but a few of them are away on a message through Edinburgh direction, won't be back till tomorrow. What's up then? You were a bit mysterious on the phone.

~ I know. Sorry about that, but you never do know who's earywigging, I say, and he smiles and nods and lights a smoke.

~ You think Shuggs will show face then? I say, and he frowns.

~ I got one of the boys to call him, tell him he's not in the firing line for this, that you want to see him, bury the hatchet as you might say. That's ten past seven now. We'll soon see. Fancy a drink then? he says and we head for the bar and it's all going very slow and peaceful and civil, like it really is someone's birthday or something.

With Gramps and his boys settled at the bar, the others having a quick knockabout at the snooker table, I grab the chance to get Danny.

~ Everything sorted then? I say, and she's smiling and nodding right away as she passes me the cigarette packet.

~ All there, plus the change. Gerry and Kelly went down to see the lads, but Josie was away. They told Maxo, and he's well up for it, should be here any minute. He said he'll try and get the Thompsons as well, so maybe half a dozen, I don't know.

~ Good. Here, you'd best take these now, I say, and turn from the eyesight of all and pull the bubble-pack of Double-Zeds from the wee box.

~ These for the others as well? she says, and I nod.

The box is fairly abulge what with the Hard O's, Whammers, Freshpops and Yelloids, but it's as well to have a fair selection of these just in case, always handy for calming the more excitable members, of whom there will surely be several.

The squeak of the swing-door alerts us, and it's Quasi the doorman who enters, followed by Shuggs and the two Jays who are inseparable friends individually named Jimbo and Jerso. The tension is snappable right away, and I see Gramps motioning with palm to his nephews, both of whom were heavily involved on the night I got my little present from Shuggs.

All eyes on me now, I suppose, so I walk over calm and smiling, and Shuggs walks very slowly towards the bar, looking square at the centre of the snooker table, as if examining the possible shots, his two henchmen close and positively wobbling with white fear.

~ Glad you could come, Shuggs, I say, and he gives me the once over before offering his hand.

~ You look good, Suzy. Very good.

~ Yeah. Save it for afters. So you know what this is all about?

~ Not in like detail, he says, and he's smiling twinkly with pupils akimbo so it's a fair bet he's downed something on the road down from the Cherry basket, but he's making just a wee bit too much movement legs and arms-wise for my liking, and I position myself accordingly.

Shuggs wouldn't be mad enough to start anything in here, but I just hope it was a calmer he dropped. And the two Jays are stuck side-by-side as if connected Siamese-style, and it's a fair bet they've only accompanied Shuggs with the very severest of reservations, but they don't appear too freaked, and the likelihood is that Shuggs has forbidden any early-evening consumption until the lie of the land is established. I reflect that their appearance shows Shuggs and friends in a new and not unflattering light – if the shoes were other-foot-wise, I would have very serious doubts about making such a visit.

I notice Quasi shifting to the far end of the bar, and Declan is looking at him, then me, then Shuggs and his boys, and maybe he's getting a picture of his place turning into some kind of battle zone 'cos I notice him reach in beside the till and that's where he's got his wee like emergency buzzer, but he must have a code for using it 'cos when Dave walks in it's like very cautious and slow, and I invite Shuggs and his lads to help themselves to the grub which dearest Miss Danny has now revealed in all its splendidness, and they cross over slow and gallus, taking defensive peeks at the assembled Pinks as they do so. Gramps catches my eye and winks.

Twenty minutes later we're all sat at the scattered low tables and Josie and Maxo have indeed managed to turn up with another couple of U-block residents – Anwar is a boozing ex-amateur boxer in his forties who stays at the block in between jail spells, and Pizza is another new character to me, a small and very worried looking deaf and dumb guy who sticks by Anwar's side and smokes non-stop. Kieran has turned up with his brother, Alto, and it's altogether a fearsome looking assembly.

All partake of the grub on offer, and the new bar lad is doing a grand job of keeping all glasses well stocked and bottles replenished as and when, and I'm just about to start the meeting when I notice a distinct aroma of turd, and I ask Danny and she nods, and it's like Chinese whispers then, all present sniffing and looking about them and generally upset by the strengthening stench.

~ Has anyone stepped in something on the way in? asks Gramps in a very loud and stern manner and this sets all checking their shoe-soles and shaking heads, then Anwar mutters something to Maxo, gets up very quickly, and hops outside with a jobby-infested jogging boot bobbing in the air, and he receives a loud cheer of derision mixed with relief and celebration, and his humiliation acts as an unexpected but very welcome ice-breaker.

But my anxiety over where to start and how to say what I have to say proves baseless. Harry Pink pipes up with what he's found out, and it sets all brows afurrow.

~ That SS on the window means it's Shaws right enough. The She Shaws.

This provokes nervous laughter. Sounds like he has a speech impediment rather than any useful information. Even Gramps chuckles, as does Harry, but he's not finished yet.

~ Their patch is Battleplace and Newgrange. There's about three, maybe four hundred of them. They do most damage in Shawhill but they don't have much serious competition otherwise till you get to Castleridge and Nitsfield. Hard to say what they're into these days, but for sure they've got all the hash carriers sewn up and they keep it cheap. Their number one used to be a private cab car owner called Prentice, but he got shot in that hassle in Priestly last Christmas. Don't know who's in charge now. They got the blame of a few murders last year, but from what I hear it's like the papers have got it in for them and there's never been any convictions of members in connection with the killings. I asked about a bit today, called the guy who'll be meeting us tonight, and he says they're heavily into controlling the smack traffic. Seems like you can't deal anywhere in their patch without getting a serious tanking, and even the users down thereabouts know not to look to buy in the area. But it's not like they sell. They don't. They just seem to have this thing about junk in the area. Mind you, at the price they set the hash at, there must be a fortune in it. You know yourselves, any smoke here-abouts is standard price, but it's nearly all bought Southside.

~ It still doesn't explain why they were up here, I say, and it's Shuggs who kind of raises a hand like he's back in school or something, and with all eyes turning to him he sort of shrinks in the seat and stares at my table.

~ This name, She-Shaws. Does that mean they're all lassies? he asks, and it seems a reasonable enquiry.

Harry shakes his head slowly.

~ When they started, yeah, but that was like early seventies or something. Like I say, we're talking hundreds of them, but that's only in the past like three, four years. It used to be a hard core of thirty, maybe fifty at most. Some of the top faces are lassies, but overall it's maybe a fifty fifty split.

~ What about these murders then? asks Gramps.

Harry shrugs, frowns, lights another fag.

~ It's a bit weird you know, it's like the rozz came out and actually said they felt sure there was a connection with the Shaws, and you know that's just not like them, causes them all sorts of bother down the line if it turns out it was them, but even the papers jumped on it too, made out the Shaws almost certainly did in these three guys up Priestley. Right enough, the old Shaws' boss did get done there, they would have had reason, but that was 'cos he was into some property scam out the Mearns direction. The guys he was dealing with in Priestley found out he was skimming and strung him up. He was old school though, and he'd been off the scene for years as far as the Shaws were concerned. There's something not right there. The Shaws' main thing was the anti-roads camp up at the edge of the estate, you know, that bit where there was the protest about the South-West by-pass. The Shaws were like the protection for the protestors. They went in team-handed a good few times when the sheriff's boys were trying to clear the camp and they made a right mess of those guys, weighed in with crowbars and blades of all descriptions, but no firearms at all. That anti-road camp should have been cleared years ago but it was the Shaws held them back so long. Cost a lot of people a lot of dosh.

~ What would be in that for them? I ask, and Harry smiles.

~ The Shaws got extra members, a right good rumble with the rozz, and the campers managed to hold that road up an awful lot longer than anyone thought they would. Ended up the security guys they sent in to finally clear it was all ex-army and hard as fuck, that's how serious they took them. If you ask me, the rozz and the press and the council and just about everybody else had good reason to get shot of that camp, and to do that they had to get rid of the Shaws. With the support they had, even with the local folk, it was never going to be a scoosh, so fingering them for the Priestley murders must've seemed a good way of turning opinion about, only everyone who's anyone down there knows that the McCanns and the Gormleys were doing each other in just the same as they've always been. It was business as usual.

~ How does Joanne come into all of this? I ask, and that's when Harry shuts up shop and shakes the noggin, clueless.

There's no way that scarred lass and her entourage turned up at my door by chance. I've never had anything to do with them, and neither, as his presence here tonight confirms, has Shuggs. He's probably feeling as threatened as I am. I find that I'm looking at him, and when his eyes come up and meet mine I know he's about to speak.

~ Joanne was dying when we got to her. I'm not trying to say we couldn't have stopped it. Maybe we could have. But that's a serious outfit, whoever it is. They had guns.

~ Were they girls? I ask, and he shakes his head.

~ We never got that close, and they were pretty well wrapped up, hats, scarves. Five of them, and Joanne. I'd say they were all guys.

~ Sure? I say.

~ The ones who moved towards us, they were definitely blokes. Big, broad, definitely guys. The others, beside Joanne, it's possible they were lassies, but I'm sure that was a squad of guys, and definitely no-one like this lassie with the scar.

~ Did Joanne say anything? I ask, and it's what I wanted to ask him from the moment he walked in the door, and he knows it.

~ She just said one thing over and over, but it was pretty hard to make out if she was just away with it, or if she knew anything what she was saying or what.

~ What did she say? I repeat, and the urge to gush is growing but I can't. Not now, here.

~ She just kept saying, get Suzy, you've got to get Suzy. That was it, he says, and his head stays low.

I don't know if it's just sheer rage or maybe guilt, but I want to kill Shuggs there and then. That it should be him to hear that, if indeed that is what he heard, makes me get to my feet, and Declan's boys step away from their observatory stance at the bar and Declan himself is watching like a hawk, but I stay where I am and cast my stare over all seated, at Gramps and Harry and my little ladies, at anyone bar Shuggs, who remains with head bowed, stroking the bottle in his hands.

~ Get Suzy, I say, very quiet, but there's a wobble again and my teeth are clenched.

Gramps looks up at me and raises a palm, perhaps fearing I'm about to flip.

~ You can take that different ways pal, he says, and I know what he means but what use is splitting hairs now, what use are those last words of hers when they can be split at all.

~ I'm telling you now, all of you, I'm telling you as straight and true and cross my heart as I can, I did not do Joanne. She was my friend and I loved her and I would never hurt her in my life. I would've walked the world for her. Yeah, we fell out. Yeah, she hated what I was doing. I don't know why she was at the Maggie that night, and I don't know any more than anyone here why she was done or why anyone would want to do her. And maybe this is madness, but I'm not drunk and I'm not whammed, but I swear it, I swear it on my life, I will find the fucker who did her. I will find him, and when I find him I will kill him. That's why I've got you all here tonight. I've got cash.

Before I know it I've gone against every sensible bone in me and taken the plastic envelopes from inside the jerkin and I'm holding them up like some great golden fleece and you can virtually see lights switch on in every set of eyes and the silence suddenly becomes like charged and sparkly.

~ I'll pay well for help. I want to go tonight. Who's up for it then?

The silence grinds on, and Harry lights a fag and Gramps is looking at his kin and Josie is looking at Gerry and Declan is at the bar with his lads afront him, still wound-up and ready to clear us all out. I know that none of the Pinks will go without the consent of Gramps, and Josie and his crowd are perhaps a better bet. But the first voice comes from the table across, and it belongs to Shuggs.

~ I'm up for it, he says, and he holds my stare as he drains the dregs from the bottle, and then the other voices come, from Maxo and Josie and Harry and sundry others, and glasses are clinked and a rumble of excitement and hate goes about the room like one of those Mexican-wave things and now I can enjoy a beer as we get our skulls together and sketch out a plan of attack. I drop a Whammer and two yelloids, sit back, close my eyes, and try to imagine South side by night.

It takes Gramps one call to sort transport, but he won't be coming along for the ride.

~ I'm sure me and some of the troops can manage to hang on here till closing time. Think you'll make it back by then? he asks, and I nod.

Shuggs is suddenly beside me. I indicate the vacant end of the bench and he sits.

~ What about tools? he asks, and I hear Gramps sort of groan.

~ Shuggs, I know you're keen, I say, but as it is we're going to be moving team-handed into an area none of us know. If we get stopped there'll be enough explaining to do, but if we're tooled it'll be a right long week-end for one and all.

~ How do we know where we're going then? asks Shuggs, and it's Gramps who leans forward.

~ Harry knows it well. He was married to that one long enough to end up knowing every hidey-hole there is. He'll keep you right. But, Suzy, I can't let the others go. Harry wants to help, so you're welcome to him, but I don't want the boys involved. You know how it is.

Indeed I do. The rozz grab every chance to hassle the Pinks as it is, despite their being involved in no greater heaviness, for the most part, than re-set and bulk baccy transport from the continent. As the head of the family he gets all the flak if anything goes wrong, from the ladies of the Pinkston household as well as the rozz, and it's probably a bit of gamble he's taking even letting me have Harry. And the alibi could be very useful, especially since I know Declan will also back me, and the private snooker lounge is not connected to the vidder apparatus covering the rest of the premises, so we only have to use the back door and be discreet.

~ So what do I do with this then? says Shuggs, pulling a short-bladed black handled mini-Bowie.

Gramps leans forward and covers it with his hand.

~ You can leave it here son, he says, and you can tell your buddies to leave theirs too.

I look at the knife, and feel the scar on my back throb as if in recognition. Shuggs clearly notes my interest in the weapon, and sobriety flashes across him.

~ By the way, I'm sorry about, you know, about what happened.

I nod.

~ Yeah, so am I, I say, but I know that Shuggs is here on account of having a close personal interest in his own well-being, not mine, and that when this is all over, and if we're both still alive and able, there will be another time and another place and business between us will be completed, and I know he knows it.

Shuggs joins his boys at the table where his two Jays are playing the Pinks at doubles. The van will be here any second. I finish the pint of Flash and feel it settle and glow. And I can feel Gramps' eyes on me as I watch the assembled team, and wonder if we can even get to the South side without them killing each other let alone anyone else.

~ Be careful, Suze, says Gramps, and I know he's not thinking about the She Shaws.

Twenty minutes later we take our leave via the fire exit, and find the van directly outside the door. It's one of those like baker's vans, the square sort used for removals and such, with a full-length roller door at the rear, and that's already up so we all pile in.

The rain was not forecast, not that I've been spending all day glued to weather reports, but this is most unwelcome as few of us are dressed for such inclemency, and it's battering down in authentic monsoon style, and the wind's making it into like curtains of pure dense wetness.

Tight squeeze as it is, all manage to sort of sit or else half-squat against the wobbly sides, but I stay standing at the shutter end of it with Kelly and Shuggs. Harry Pinkston is in the front with the driver, who works for Gramps, and the arrangement is that the lad will drop us wherever Harry says and the van will come back to pick us up at midnight. It's already almost half nine, so we'll have to be sharpish about locating these Shaws, wherever they may be.

I check the wad in my pocket. Might as well get the troops squared up now, the agreement being half up front and half after, but I don't want follow-up hassles so best get it over with. A ton a head, and one-fifty for Harry, Shuggs and Josie. Shuggs palms his and slips it into his pocket without checking it, which I take to be a compliment of some kind, or an example of gross stupidity. The other lads are well-pleased, and the cash seems to make them more impatient.

Kelly slowly fingers her way through the contents of the cigarette packet as a secretary might check for a file and she eventually pulls out a Whammer. She looks at me and I smile, mine already kicking in. I don't care what she does now. I would normally vet Kelly's intake very carefully, but tonight is different. When she closes the packet I tell her to pass it to Danny, which she does.

Danny is crouching against the wall to my right, and looks a tad travel-sick, but after her piggish intake of garlic bread and chopped-pork rolls in the Hall she has no-one to blame, and knows it. And I know that she knows that if we have to stop to allow her to evacuate her stomach then she will not be a popular camper. Perhaps reading my thoughts, she releases a hearty belch and looks up, grinning, as if to prove that she is alright. Maxo, who is sitting beside her, looks impressed and starts up a conversation by offering her the remnants of his joint.

Gerry and Josie are up on the platform which sits above the driver's cabin, and look quite happy, bobbling about as the van lurches and bounces, knees drawn up to their chests, laughing at jokes I can't hear and just generally being as absorbed in each other as it's possible to be when you're in van full of damp and scared people and are heading into fuck-only-knows-what.

Danny plucks a yelloid from the packet and holds it up for me to see and I nod twice, the second time at Gerry, and Danny carefully closes the packet before lobbing it up to the lovebirds. I don't know what she takes out, but she kind of points the packet at Josie and raises her eyebrows and I nod again and he gets something too, looking for every slobboid inch of him like a schoolboy going through a Christmas sock.

When the packet is thrown back, I check inside, and there's only two Whammers left in the pile of sundries, so I take them out and plank them in my breast pocket. The rest can be spread about. It's not worth getting lifted for a few poxy yelloids, so I offer the packet to Shuggs. He looks astonished, then shakes his head and pats his stomach, so I lob the packet down to Maxo and he pounces on it pronto with much laughter and wide toothless grinning.

From the shifting of the van I'm pretty sure I know where we are for the first ten minutes or so, but then the juddering and swaying sorts of levels off and we're picking up speed and must be on the toll-road South. It's maybe strange, but I feel decidedly dicky when things get smoother and I sort of squat down and try not to look too sickly, but eventually have to fold my arms on closed knees and rest my head atop.

Some folk go over the top on the Whammers, start freaking out and saying they can see God and all that stuff. Maybe they can. I've never seen him yet. It's usually more than an hour before I get anything more than a mild sort of hum, like the feeling you get when you're remembering a fight you were in, or thinking about when you had some close shave type thing and you could easily have been done in, something like that. It's not what you'd call pleasant, but maybe it depends on the sort of mood you're in to start with. And maybe the adrenalin has something to do with it as well, like maybe it interferes with it, or maybe enhances it. I don't know.

But now, slumped against the like extremely uncomfortable bending corrugated door of this shuddering van, I'm sinking into the Whammer, and it's sinking into me, and my mercury pool has gone and gravity doesn't mean a thing. It starts away down in some part of my guts, way deep inside my chest, or maybe that's the heart, and it gets heavy and thick, and it's like it's dropping through me, but I don't know if I'm the right way up and now I couldn't open my eyes if I wanted to.

The heaviness suddenly disappears, and I feel like I'm the strongest person who's ever lived. Every tiniest bit of me tingles and pulses and sort of swells, like every cell and vein and hair is showing off to its neighbour, but not like in a boastful or aggressive way, just saying hey-guys-what-about-this, and there's this total whizzing buzz of aliveness and I know that if I want to I can jump higher than I've ever jumped before, run faster, punch harder without even really trying, you name it.

But that's not to say that I want to – it's not a power thing, but more that I just know I can. And this buzz just gets harder and deeper and I can feel the ridges on the roller-door pressing against my scar, but that's no problem, and the pain is just my scar saying hello to the blades on the roller just like they said hello to Shuggs's blade that night, just like the blade that said hello to the jelly inside Joanne's eye, and it's all alright, it's all fine, and that's the feeling about the whole set-up now, about everyone in the van, everyone in Viewhill, the Magenta, the Cherry basket, the wannabes and nerrdowells shifting in the darkness on the brewery-path, and the rozz in the Spring, and it's like it's just not possible anymore to feel anything but love for every-thing and anyone, and they're all just like merged into this big ball along with the van and the road we're on, and the rain tapping on the fibreglass roof, and the smell of damp clothes is the same smell as damp grass in summer, and that's the same as the white sand on the beach up North when I was five and Dad was there and that's the same smell as the skin of the frog I kept in my room for three days before Mum found out and Ollie's snack-boxes come in there as well, and it's like this big merging ball can't take any more so it bursts, faster and louder than anything that's ever happened, even your big bang is in here, along with all the other big bangs that ever were or will be, and they're like just the baby of this thing, and the light that comes out of it isn't like normal light, it's like solid, it's light you can make things with, so I grab hold of a tiny part if it and I make every animal programme I've ever seen, all bastard snarling hairy things getting fucked and scoffed by other bigger hairier things and climbing up trees to get away from even bigger and much hairier things and then falling into bright green water and swimming right into the middle of the world, and then all the laughs I've ever heard come up all at the same time, all made with this light and all like coming together, and this makes this great thunder-laugh like an earthquake that holds everything, all the furniture and clouds I've ever seen, and all the joints I've smoked and the Whammers and the yelloids and the sunsets and the snowflakes on tight skin, and I must be so far away now that I know I have to get back, and I have to say fuck-it to myself to try and snap away from it, and I must make some kind of reaching out movement with my hand cos then there's this like crack of electricity, just like a plug going into a socket, and the light kind of melts and scatters inside my eyes, just like mercury would, and it drops into my guts and settles into a pool and I know I'm back the right way up, and I get my eyes open and there's still light melting, but when it does and the greys and blacks and blues come up dark and shadowy, and Shuggs is sort of slumped beside me, half-asleep himself, and my hand is on his arm, wet cold fabric of his jacket stuck to my fingers and the van is juddering hard and bouncing again and slowing down, a great shivery shaky shudder sparks along my toes then runs full and strong through every muscle and nerve and makes me kind of gasp out when it hits my head, and all I want to do is find the Shaws and get this sorted once and for all and get home to my bed and sleep for days.

It's strange how people just sort of assume that someone else will take charge, like tell them what to do. Shuggs is kind of looking at me as the van stops, and it sinks in that I still haven't really told anyone what's going on. As far as anyone knows we're out for a bit of a wander, there might be a scrap, but that's about it, and most have enough booze or whatever in them now not to really care that much. It takes me a second or two to get my lips and tongue moving what with them being sort of half-frozen, but when I start the troops all perk up nice, wide eyes and open ears as they zip up jackets and pull on their bunnets and what-not.

~ Listen up folks, we've only maybe a couple of hours max here. Harry's pal will show us where these folk might be. Chances are nothing heavy will happen, so don't get involved unless you have to. Don't split up. Stick with your own, get strung out a fair bit, but keep each other in sight.

I have to stop then, my throat suddenly dry as can be without warning, so I hack and cough in true smokers mode for what feels like a minute and Kelly slaps my back which doesn't help and my face flushes that way I hate and then I'm okay again just as Jimbo pipes up.

~ What if the rozz pick us up then? he asks, and it's a fair one.

~ You're on a job for the Commissioner's Office, I snap out brief and fast, and that's it. If you get a hard time just stick it out, the usual. If it comes right down to it give them my name and I'll put you through the books as casual and that'll fling it back to me. Don't worry about the rozz.

I know I'm really just making it all up, but there's no option now and even if I say so myself it does come out good, like I've done this a hundred times before. There's a general mumbling which sounds broadly approving of it all, and I suppose that's when I get the chance to really think about what's happening. No more Joanne, Mum, Viewhill, rozz. The job in hand looms large, with only the roller-door between us and a new place with new dangers and strangers. I've never been very much into gassing about Fate and all that kismet-related stuff, but sometimes I suppose you sort of snap awake and wonder how the hell you ended up in certain situations, and maybe it's the Whammer, but I get that feeling now, and if you sat me down and asked me to explain what the fuck I'm up to I wouldn't know where to start.

A saying about fishes and pond sizes flashes into my head, and the Whammer buzz briefly returns, with pictures of dark dolphins and whales and suchlike all giving it nose-down and disappearing into thick watery black silence. Then there's a bastard of a bang and rattle, and the shutter-door rolls up like a blind on a window. There's a wall of wet wind and noise of blustery traffic slooshing nearby, and we raise our collars and lower our bunnet-brims and jump like paratroopers into the Southside night.

CHAPTER TEN

I can probably count on one hand the number of times I've been South of the river, so I haven't the faintest where we are. Harry's had the van parked in this really narrow lane, front facing the street and a darkened tenement, and conveniently defective street-lighting providing fair cover as we drop onto the muddy gravel path.

Truth be told, I get a nasty shiverish turn when I drop out of the van and look about, this path being situated in between a tall black gable on one side, and an avenue of mature and tightly packed fir trees on the other, only the tiniest patch of second-hand orange light managing to find its way through to us via a reflecting window somewhere on the tenement. The lane appears to narrow into the darkness as it heads quite steeply uphill, and I have to quell the fearful notion that Gramps would allow us to be driven into strange territory with anyone he doesn't completely trust.

The guy talking to Harry when we get out is small

and about forty, soaked through and very pissed-off looking. Harry passes him the cash I gave him earlier, a ton, and he checks it close with eyes ascrew in the dimness. Harry looks about, beckons me.

~ He wants more, he says.

From the wad in my pocket I peel off the outer note. In the light the silvery two-zero glints but he's already seen it so I pass it and he manages a smile of sorts.

~ I'll take you to within sight of the close and that's it, he says.

~ Whose close? I ask, and he kind of sniggers and pauses.

As I've just handed over an undeserved bonus, I'm not prepared to start having a game of call-my-bluff with this little man, so I take a step back, quick breath in, then bring my left boot up in a flick which only just touches his right shin. He collapses, howling, and I'm down squatting afront him, a fistful of anoraked hair, other hand out palm-flat and fingers at his neck. I speak low, and am aware that the disembarked team are now gathered about.

~ Because you know Harry here, you can have the twenty I just gave on top of the ton you got, but if you even hint that you're expecting more I'll kick you unconscious and take it all back along with your nuts as a souvenir. Understand?

I release the wretch so he can answer, but he simply folds back in on his own torso, and only some very serious cajoling from Harry gets him back upright, and he hops on one foot as he apologises.

~ No bother. Honest, no problem. I wasn't going to say a thing anyway. Look, I live here you know, I just don't want to get too near and that.

~ So whose close is it? I ask again, and he gasps again before answering.

~ Emma. Emma Jack.

~ Big bitch? I say then, scar down the middle of her coupon?

He gets an attack of wide-eyes then, the leg-pain forgotten in the panic he's now experiencing.

~ That's not Emma, he says, and then more silence.

So the Whammer must have been well and truly absorbed because then I'm on top of the runt and Harry is trying to pull me off but I've my hands about the bastard's throat and my thumbs are pressing into his windpipe and I am going to do him right now. I pull my hands away and hold them up and open, fingers splayed, afront his bloated wee face.

~ Name. Now.

~ Penny. Penny B, he says.

~ Who's Emma?

~ She's the number two. It's her flat. I don't know where Penny's place is exactly. Somewhere up Shawbridge way but I don't know. Honest to Christ, on my wean's life, I don't know.

~ And will this Penny be there then? I say as I get up, and he stays exactly where he is, arms still flat by his side on the muddy driveway.

~ That's where they hang out week-ends. They should be there with this rain on.

~ I hope so, I say, and then I help Harry to haul the wee chancer to his feet and I stare at him and he turns, and we all follow, silent on the wet grass.

The lane gets so dark heading away from the street that I whisper forward to Harry to stop, which he does, and I tell him to get a hold of the runt guide, and keep hold, and reach out behind and it's a male hand and with only silhouette I have to ask who it is and it's Shuggs, and he says he never knew I cared and I tell him to get the next in line and pass it on and soon we're off again, a congo-line in darkness, like nursery kids on a day out in the country, slipping in the mud as the path trails off and we're making our way through what maybe used to be allotments or such, but is madly over-grown with stumpy hedges and many treacherous objects such as protruding corners of corrugated iron sheeting, discarded drain-pipes and sundry other garbage, and the smell of like a thousand cats is all about and it occurs that all our good new gear will be mightily distressed by the time we get through this like quagmire of filth.

A low slimy brick wall has to be negotiated, after which the back-court lights of a skyline-cutting tene-ment help enough so that the awkwardness of hand-holding is over and we can see enough to lightly bunch. Then we've another, higher wall to climb, and that's two by two, into the back-court of this obviously well-derelict tenement with old security signs hanging here and there claiming that dogs are on patrol, but the little runt guide is out front so he must know otherwise, and now that we're away from the many trees the rain can get to us again, and it does so with the help of the wind, stronger as we climb the hill. Then its just across an overgrown back-court to the rear entrance of this long-empty building, with its shiny steel window boards and torrents of rainwater dropping from smashed gutters, and into a close where the door has been blasted off by the desperate roofless, and the smell of another thousand different cats hits us as we slide and skid through accumulated waste of beasts and humans alike.

I make my way to the front, where the runt guide has stopped and is peeking through the gap at the side of the huge steel door.

~ We've got to get onto the main drag now, he says, there's no other way. It's five minutes hoof down to the Cross, then another two hundred yards by that. I could give you the address.

The thin bar of streetlight coming through the gap shows enough of my face for him to know that his suggestion is not acceptable, so he resigns himself to making an effort on the door, but it takes another three of us to heave and haul and force enough of a gap so that the troops can slide through one by one, and it takes about six of us to create a gap large enough for Maxo to negotiate.

We get onto the main drag, and I can't place where the van must be now. We're at the very peak of the hill, and there's some kind of monument with a statue of this long-dead punter on top which puts me briefly in mind of the battle of the George, but we've soon left it behind and are marching down the steep hill, and there are bodies here and there, running to and from pubs or home or whatever, keen to get out of the pounding rain but hurried no doubt by the sight of this anxious-looking squad descending towards the Cross at some speed.

Past a garage, bright and busy, a wee man is selling the Big Issue, and we all pile past without word and he does not declare his homelessness nor ask us to purchase his wares. Past a pub, and heads at the windows turn.

The traffic starts to thicken, but no rozz visible as yet. A taxi-rank, several cars waiting, but the first pulls away as we near, passengerless, and the second follows suit. The third cabbie doesn't even realise he's now in pole position until he looks up from his paper and we're nearly on him and I see him scramble for his key and the engine farts into life and the blackness of the exhaust is still billowing as we leave him behind and reach the Cross itself, which is the meeting point for many pubs and eating-houses of cosmopolitan variety.

We're forced to wait for the green man thanks to the sheer weight of traffic now, and as we do so the hungry punters in the Italian pizza house gawp, then focus with spectacular intensity on their garlic bread and pasta and the waiters walk into each other as the wee green man flashes up and we march on, soaked to the skin and grim of face.

It is probably fair to assume that our presence has been well noted by the traders of the area by the time we pass the busiest part of the Cross and head down a slightly dipping hill which is flanked by two long rows of clean and tidy tenements. The road is nice and broad and level so that you can see whoever might be about from a distance, and further down this street, maybe two hundred yards from the Cross, the light of a late-night shop spills onto the otherwise shaded pavement.

The runt suddenly stops, and turns, looking for me.

~ See the chippie? he says, and I nod. It's the first close past it. Three up. That's Emma's place. Please, can I go now? Please?

I wave my hand at him without even catching his eye, and he vanishes up the nearest close, where I very much doubt he actually lives. A pull at my jacket. It's Danny, her new smart togs completely stuck to her, and her new hair-do washed away. Eyes asquint, she's peering down the street at the block indicated.

~ There's lights on alright, she says, and I don't even try to follow her gaze, half-blinded as I am by rain.

She steps another pace ahead of me, and we're as plain as day, bunched on the pavement afront a closed newsagent shop with the blue neon of the off-sales beside it lighting the pavement behind us.

~ Just by the post-box, look, and Danny is pointing and I follow her finger to see two figures standing at the close-mouth, their heads visible above the line of the hedge, and they're looking at us, no doubt about it. It's the same close the runt guide mentioned, so what is this? A guard? Or maybe they saw us on the way down and managed to get back just ahead of us.

So we move off again, and slower now, with rain still pounding down and the wind against us as we get to the next corner, and we're just one block away from the suspected Shaws' base on the other side of the road. A vehicle behind, but a swift check and it's okay, just an exhaust-weary Vauxhall schlooshing through the swimming street, and it speeds up as it passes. We crowd into a bus shelter, and mightily crammed it is too, and there's this like aroma of mushrooms coming off us what with the dampness and the sweat and the adrenalin, and a strange smell we make as well as a strange sight.

Harry and Kieran and Alto look well-pished and tired, and maybe it's the intake of oxygen, or maybe the unexpected traipse over the back of the hill, but whatever it is, they don't look up for this at all and it shows. Josie is sticking like glue to Gerry, and with Maxo,

Pizza and Anwar square behind them they appear fairly
solid. Shuggs is smiling despite the awful whiteness of
the two Jays, and I can see now that there is something
a bit mad about him right enough. Kelly is sniffing like
her life depends on it in between massive deep breaths,
and Danny, despite the tragic loss of her new image, is
as sound as ever and looks ready for anything.

We're unlucky weather-wise, but this is as good a
squad as I could have hoped for so no point dallying
further. I instruct Shuggs, and he nods and grins, and
passes orders to Jimbo, who listens most attentively
before striding out, most gallus it has to be said, along
the pavement until he is squarely opposite the chippie.

My eyes dry now, I can see the bay window three-up
above the chippie fill as Jimbo stands with back to
them, briefly scans the window of the closed grocer's,
then takes out his can and sprays a large Cherry hiero on
the roller-shutter. The agitation in the figures occupying
the bay-window is immediate and dramatic, and the
bodies disperse to leave only one. It might be her. Penny.

Jimbo is half-jogging back to us when the first sign of
the attack comes, but not from the target flat. A door
slamming echoes from the next close down on our side
of the street, and quickly follows the scliffing and
stomping of footsteps hammering downstairs, and they
come belting out into the middle of the street and we
move into the openness of the road and we're roaring
and they're roaring and the bodies spill from the close
beside the chippie and we've got the scrap we came
looking for alright.

Sometimes I get folk asking me how I can remember
all the fights I've been in. It's like they think I'm maybe

just making it all up or trying to make it more dramatic than it actually was or I'm just purely a liar and that's that, and it gets me very mad, so it does.

It's like, you take a great chess champion, or it doesn't even have to be a champion, there's loads of folk who're right into it, and they can remember every game they've played in competitions, and not only can they remember their own moves but also the moves of their opponents, and then there's the real like top champions of champions who go on like tours, exhibitions, and they can play like a whole room full of lesser champions, but still great players mind you, and they can even remember all the moves of all the games, and even do it with a fucking blindfold on. You don't get folk saying they don't believe that, mainly cos I suppose it's all down there in the record books and you can check it if you want, and even if they've got wee holes in the blindfolds or whatever, it's still pretty amazing that they can remember all that stuff.

So why can't folk believe the same about fighting? Maybe I'm biased, but I think if someone's coming at you with a knife or a baseball bat or they've got big steelie boots on and you have to fight them, that's maybe something you'd remember just as much as where you moved a rook or a pawn or some wee fucking horse thing.

It's all about being awake I suppose. Not just awake like as in the opposite of asleep, but really, really wide awake, sparkly open and ready. Whammers, Zip and Flash aside, I've always been able to get solidly full-awake when bother is on. Now and then you can lose it, but that's more to do with the old Viking approach, when you get razzled up to the eyeballs on magic potions and foaming at the gob and all that stuff, and I think sometimes maybe, what with my Scandinavian blood from Mum's side and all, maybe there's some of that berserker stuff in me right enough. No doubt there's plenty to be said in its favour when things get rough. But I'd prefer to see myself as a professional, someone who's listened and learned and can do it properly. I don't want to think that it's all about being mad and rabid and ready to kill at the drop of a hat. It's more to do with keeping your wee mercury pool calm and knowing that your arms and legs and sundry other body parts will do exactly what you want them to when you want them to.

So, as far as this particular scrap goes, I know I'll remember it all. Me and Joanne used to talk about it quite often, the idea that very small actions can change your life, and particularly in fights. So you throw a jab when you can stay still, and they go underneath with a knife and you're dead. You kick too high on a slippery surface, balance goes, you're down on your arse, a heel scrapes your ear right off. Well, those are the kind of small actions I was more interested in, whereas Joanne was always on about like bumping into someone you haven't met for ages and you end up meeting for a drink and at that night out you meet someone who offers you a job etc, etc. It's the same principle I suppose, only on a different sort of time scale. She used to wonder if there was any way of finding out when those moments would come, cos then you really would be able to enjoy life, you'd know what was coming, what choices to make. So it's obvious now that she never did find a way of doing it, and I wonder if maybe, in those few seconds before the knife broke through her skin afront the Maggie, if maybe she had time to think about the decision she made that had brought her there, and whether or not there was any time for regret.

And what of this moment for me? Is this maybe the big fight I've always imagined I would have one day? The one where I get to fight for my life for real? If not, it's looking very much like a contender.

Perhaps I should keep Gerry a bit closer, or perhaps Gerry should keep a bit closer to me, but she gets very quick when she starts, and never has she had much bother in the past so I'm not over-worried when she strikes out in front with Maxo and Josie close by, and she's clearly opted to deal with those on our side of the road as I peel off to attract those from the chippie-close.

We, that is, me, Danny and Shuggs and the two Jays, form a wobbly line which falls back on its ends to make a rough circle when the collision comes, and it works pretty well. There is fear and confusion on the faces before us, mostly about ages with me, and fit and fast but more into the rituals and the gestures rather than the old one-two, and they fall back a bit as the first contacts are made and they know they're not dealing with puppy-rubbers. Six of them altogether from the chippie-close, and although I haven't time to turn about and count there must be another five at least from the opposite close, and it sounds like they're all chaps.

Two bodies first, both shortish males, at and about my front, another two skipping about Shuggs and the Jays, and there's one heftier chap behind trying to take the piss out of Danny with very picturesque kicks which she simply steps back from, as is her usual style. One of mine comes in close enough, wide-eyed and screaming blue abuse at me through the rain and he's shuffling about making a lot of noise, but then I know the heftier fellow is coming at me from the back so a swift turn, bend and fire out the kick and it catches him good just at the hip and he goes down in a messy tumble with Danny rugby-kicking his ribs as he hits the deck, and that's him out of the way immediate-wise.

The dancer afront me is still going through his repertoire when reinforcements emerge from the chippie-close, and even a split-second glance shows this to be the heavy team, walking calm and tooled, so best get the wee ones out the road first, but Shuggs beats me to the time-waster with a crunching jarler-boot and he flops over like a burst balloon, curling into a ball as he drops.

Kelly's screams rise high above the general din, but this is a good sign, and woe betide the recipient of her wrath as the heavier team split and set about helping their weaker fellows, and the one who nears us is a beast, upwards of fifteen stone easy, and similar build to me but a good three inches taller. From her face I'd say she's drunk, but given that she wields a rather nasty looking cleaver-type implement, this is small consolation, so I check my back quickly before devoting my very fullest attention to her.

Danny is directly behind me, so I wait for this biggest of Berthas to make her move and it comes fast enough, a low swoop with the steel but it's nowhere near and I don't even have to move, and when she pulls the arm back again I step forward and kick my height and the steel toe catches her directly under her square chin and there's a clacking of teeth and she topples directly back, flat out on the pavement and that's much easier than I'd hoped for so back round again to find that Danny is being set upon by two small creatures, one of indeterminate sex, and is having trouble removing a pair of hands from her crowning glory as was, so a couple of hooks and she's free and I leave her to finish them off, but somehow I've allowed one of the heavier members to get behind me, and I'm first made aware of this slip when I feel like a gunshot in the middle of my back and I'm on the deck and it must've been quite a kick from this small lass, and she's hammering on the back of my neck, so very quickly hands over and behind, but the hair is well-greased, so find the ears and a good tight grip, some neck-skin too, and up and over with her and she slams down, still clawing and trying to knee my face, and she's a wild one right enough so up on feet again as she slips out and one crack to her jaw and a kick to the guts, and Shuggs suddenly appears from nowhere to bring a swift boot into her forehead so she's out of commission as well.

A quick scan, and it looks alright. Kelly is busy with a tall goatee-bearded fellow who has a long stick, not a baseball bat, not a fashioned item of any kind, just a long thick stick, and he's kind of waving it about but she's diving in low and sharp between swoops of this thing and hacking short sharp kicks at his shins, like she's chopping down a tree. Kieran and Alto look busy enough, pummelling methodical and hard into a couple of bodies which have like sunk into this hedge just around the corner from the chippie, and judging by the howling issuing therefrom it seems that they are doing alright. Danny grunts and I turn to see that she's got another two hopping in a circle about her, and I get the one with back turned to me and Danny lumbers after the other as Shuggs and his boys turn to the heavier lads who accompanied the big Bertha.

Gerry and Josie are side-by side, trading conventional blows with a couple of handy-looking guys, but these lads must note the odds stacking as Anwar and Pizza approach, and so back off towards the chippie-close, glancing up at the window where there is now no-one. A scream, I turn, and Kelly has felled the goatee-beard, and is raining celebratory kicks on his hand-shielded face. Maxo arrives to haul her off, and then another scream, and it's Josie, and Gerry is down, even though the lads they had been scrapping have now scarpered up the close.

Josie's on knees, face almost touching the deck as he talks to her, but to look at Gerry's horrible position now, legs twisted like they may be broken, head hard against the road as if she's listening out for something, it looks bad, so bad.

We get over and I have to pull Danny off, then Josie. I turn her over, and she's already dead. At first I don't even see the knife, but when I try to unzip her jerkin, the zip jams where the black blade is firm and deep, right under the sternum. I look up and Kelly's looking down, and then she's off, heading for the close, screaming so high it is barely audible. Shuggs takes off after her with Danny, and they manage to drag her away before she gets the glass panel completely kicked in.

Danny howls at the empty window above. Josie's hands are riveted to Gerry's jacket. She's like spasming, but it's only nervous stuff, and you can tell by her eyes that she's gone. It's no use, and I tell him, and I tell them all, but Josie is gone, totally gone, unblinking, dry-eyed and unreachable. And Gerry is definitely dead. The sirens are still far away.

A sudden rush of booted feet, and turning, there's

Harry and Kieran and Alto making retreat of rapid variety back towards the Cross.

~ Come on! is the shout from Harry.

Everything freezes and is clear. Josie will stay. No doubt about that. Gerry's killer went up that close, that much we all saw. The Pinks are already at the Cross, but the chances are they'll get lifted, having nowhere decent to hide until they get up that bastard hill, and they're in no fit state to do that pronto.

I let Josie hold Gerry close, get myself up. Nearer and nearer, but not moving fast, the rozz are maybe stuck on the main drag, this being a traffic-controlled residential area spaghettied with many one-way arrangements and dead-ends.

Nearing Shuggs and Danny, who are being assisted by the two Jays in their efforts to control the hysterical Kelly, I see the wound on her neck from ten feet away, a deep and bloodless slash down her left cheek which will take much stitching. But she probably doesn't even know it's there, and it's certainly not why she's freaking. Gerry was her friend. Best she stays, as a period of rozz-custody will lessen the chances of her killing someone and they'll get the wound seen to.

Shouts from the Cross, and the blue light pulsing off the buildings suggests that Harry and friends are in trouble just like I thought, and at the other end of the street we're on, which ends at a darkened park of some sort where the tenements end, fresh sirens are growing louder. Kelly is flat on her back, jerking and thrashing her head from side to side, and Shuggs is standing back now, white and confused with his boys by his side.

Time to go, but there's no way we'll make much progress staying as a squad, and from one glance at

Danny I know she's thinking the same. There's nothing else we can do here, and the others will have to fend for themselves. I grab Danny's arm, haul her away from Kelly, then make for the side-street where the body of one of the Shaws is protruding from a large hedge.

It's a tree-lined curvy street packed with many cars semi pavement-parked, and old style wall-fastened lights which are helpfully dim, and we're belting along it keeping an eye out for any open closes as the blue lights start beating through the trees and doors slam and now they're arriving in force. Josie must have stayed with Gerry right enough, and God only knows what's happened to Shuggs and the Jays, but Maxo and Anwar are close behind us as Danny tries another close, and it's yet another fast-shut glass number, but she steps back and heels the bottom panel out with one kick and there's room enough there to scurry under, Danny first, then me, and the giant Maxo is having much bother fitting his shoulders through this space as the running rozz close up right behind, but no point in us all getting nabbed so I urge Danny on and thank fuck the back door is open, and we're through there and across the garden, up and over a low wall and another garden, a locked door, up and over again and trust there to be this drunk arse letting his small terrier-type dog out for a pish, and he's pishing himself, and his whole face seems to like open up when he sees us piling over his wall and he starts calling on sundry neighbours to help him and he makes a bid for me, but he's so hammered that I run around him and leave him sprawling and cursing in the wet grass and go belting out after Danny who's already in the close, then this wee white Scottie thing gets a hold of my ankle as I'm jumping up the stairs, and although it bites mostly into the upper part of my ankle-boot, it sort of snaps off for a half-instant and re-attaches itself right about the back of my calf and there's a wrench and I know it's hurt me before I manage to slap it off and it drops onto the grass still snarling and yapping at high pitch along with its owner.

Out of the close, and we're on another of these curvy side-streets with a wee like park in the centre with old tenements curving all about, and the gap at the end with bright glow of main streetlights is the obvious exit. The rozz will have the place sealed off in minutes, so it's as well to make a run for it now and hope we may encounter a fast black, or a much rarer but equally valuable bus.

We try to walk calm, innocent, like it's the kind of night two mud-covered lassies would just go out for a wee wander in the persisting rain, and Danny's chest is heaving and I'm feeling a tad shattered myself, but we walk nice and steady, keeping right in by the wee hedged front gardens. A rozz light approaches the end of the drag to our rear, so a swift hop into the first available close, but it passes on, and on we go.

If I wasn't lost before, I am now. This road, narrower and curvier than where the Shaws live, seems to be heading into a purely residential place, there being few signs of life and little traffic noise or lights, and the chances of hailing a hack here must be only marginally better than the likelihood of seeing a bus, which is zero. But the concentration of sirens, now joined by that of an ambulance, is such that we cannot risk heading back to the busier patch, and so we take the only course left.

The road narrows further, and the tenements are

replaced by smartish semi-detached houses of old style
with large gardens and walls and iron gates with names
and fake Victorian lamps and suchlike, and you can tell
this is a place of monied folk, with long sleek cars
sparkling wet on crunchy gravelly driveways, and trees
carved in the shape of like cartoon trees, and expensive
sounding dogs with deep rich barks sound off at us as
we plod further, and Danny is crying and sniffing and
my leg is aching more, and I know the wee dog has
done me some damage as I can feel the stickiness of the
blood in my boot and I'm fast developing a limp as it
starts to swell and tighten.

This place is like another world altogether. There's
virtually nothing moving apart from us and the trees
and the great solid blanket of orange cloud overhead,
and we can hear anything approaching well before any
lights are seen, not that there's any serious traffic to
speak of.

There are lights on in some of the houses, but even
then, there seems to be like no noise, as if they're all
watching the box with the sound turned well down, or
else maybe they're all sitting reading books or doing
crosswords or something. The main sound is the rain,
and if anything it's getting heavier, and bastard cold it
is too with the wind gusting and shaking more rain out
of the trees on top of us. I've still the two Whammers
in my pocket, and I stop and try to fish them out but
they've crumbled in the wetness and are nothing more
than a thin line of gritty paste at the bottom of the
pocket. Danny stops crying, but looks dreadful. We've
walked maybe a mile or so from the Cross when the
road dips on a long and straight drag which appears to
be a dead end, and we're maybe half-way down this

terraced avenue when the traffic signs confirm that there is indeed no passage for traffic, the road leading to some kind of footbridge.

We see the small bridge before we realise there's a river there, and it's a surprise, perhaps because we're so used to seeing roads under bridges. It must be a small and trickly thing in normal weather, but as we get closer, being ultra-cautious in case of ambush what with this being a natural place for rozz to seal off, we can see the water high and choppy, battering the steep sides of the bank and carrying debris at a fair old rate. Wading or swimming would not make us any wetter than we are, but even Danny, who's a much better swimmer than me, would not get across that. Maybe it's only thirty feet or so, but it's too fast and high and dangerous, and fuck knows where it ends up, so plod we must, across the wee chunky steel bridge, whether we like it or not.

But I don't like it, and neither does Danny. We hang back under a thick like umbrella formed by this mad overgrown hedge with ivy through it, backs to the sandstone wall which surrounds this dark-windowed like mansion of true horror story style with false castle-style turrets and great gnarly baldy trees silhouetted against the orange sky like big graspy old hands.

Danny is shivering so bad she can hardly speak, and I can feel my leg starting to seize up at the knee as well as the ankle. We can't go much further, but can't stay here unless it's hypothermia we want. The street on the other end of the bridge is where tenements start up again, and it's a long straight drag, well-lit, at the end of which there is much light and passing of tiny white and red lights indicating a heavy traffic flow, so it must be another junction of some kind, and the likeliest place now to get some form of transport. I can't see any other way out, but I still don't like it.

~ What do you think? I ask, but Danny just shakes her head and looks ready to start gushing again, so I put an arm round her and give her a quick hug which is not at all like me but she looks like she really needs it.

~ Come on, Danny, tell me what you think, I say again, and she looks at me hard, frowning.

~ You're the boss, she says, it's up to you.

~ No more bosses, I say, and sort of ranting in a quiet way I am but so tired and confused and unreasonably scared of this wee shiny bridge.

The rain seems to take on a beat, a rhythm, and Danny squats, head hanging, and I also drop, arm still about her. The beat grows, soft but rapid, and then it's maybe the wind that changes but the 'copter is clear and close, and back to our right, where we've just come from, the huge blue-white beam is slowly scanning and shifting through the rain. For a minute or so it moves nearer, and you can hear from the tone and beat of the 'copter when it's moving or hovering or whatever, and the beam is going right slow along what must be the gardens of the big houses we just passed and I know that if it's got one of those thermal seeker things on it we'll be well and truly done for, so there's nothing to be done except sit it out. Then it's gone. So suddenly, and maybe the wind took away the noise of its departure, but it's vanished, and it must be time now to make a move before exhaustion sets in. My back is pulsing with pain where I took the kick, and my leg is starting to feel like someone else's, and God only knows what sort of punishment Danny took, but I've never seen her so drained and lost.

So it's out from under the ivy hedge umbrella and down the path and we're hemmed in on both sides by high chicken-wire fencing which is probably to keep sprogs away from the river bank, but liable to cause claustrophobia in the hunted, such as we are, and then we're striding across the bridge, maybe only forty feet long it is, but bouncy underfoot, and the river is very close underneath, only a few feet, and very scary too with its speed and noise and bogging browny orange colour, and we're no more than half-way when the bastards come out from under the end of it, and without even turning about I know they're behind us as well, and Danny starts climbing the chest-high thick steel tubing fencing, and I try to haul her back, but she swings over and like teeters on the tiny ledge, holding on to the top firm, and I'm about to join her in true Butch Cassidy and Sundance Kid style and have one knee atop the rail when I turn about and there stands Penny as cool as you like, and not even that wet considering, and she's smiling and she must know that I won't jump. Not now.

CHAPTER ELEVEN

Her colleagues, two at either end of the bridge, stay put. Danny stays put. I move to the centre of the wobbly bridge and stand, waiting. And she comes with the same walk I remember from Magenta, like it's only her hips that are actually moving, and everything else is following, and I can see now that she's shorter than I thought, but still has a couple of inches on me.

She briefly raises a palm, but it's aimed at her friends behind me, and I know they're still at the end and haven't come on the bridge itself, otherwise I'd feel the footsteps through the wobbles, and she keeps coming and I get my right foot back and bring the paws up and wait for it, that kick, cos surely it's her best card, but she strides on one step further than I expect, and she's right in front of me and I feel a sudden confusion. She's just out of knee range and will surely parry any kick, so a punch must be best now, and even as I'm thinking it she pushes her face out a tad and closes her eyes.

So it's well suckered I am then, 'cos I snap out the left,

intending to follow through with the right but she's dangling string in front of a kitten, and her eyes are still shut when she parries the jab and then my lungs empty and my diaphragm locks solid and I'm tumbling arse over head and I'm struggling to breathe and can't get up. Then she's standing over me, looking down, smiling, and she closes her eyes again and laughs, and her buddies are rushing to the centre of the bridge, and then Danny screams my name and shouts go up and there's the splash of dearest big Danny hitting water and I try to shout to her but there's nothing coming out or going in and the panic is setting in and whiteness sparkles all around and my eyes are open but the whiteness becomes redness and blackness and I'm well and truly out.

When I wake up it's Danny nipping my ears, gently slapping my cheeks, and I sit up pronto, not knowing where or who or what, and it comes back piece by piece but I'm still trying to work out where the clothes came from and what the familiar but out-of-place smell is and Danny is gibbering so fast and hard that I have to cover my ears and shut my eyes and try to shake some sense back in before I can even try to speak.

My head feels as if someone has tied something thin about it just above the ears and is pulling it tighter, garrotte-style, and I rub a palm over my now dry hair and there's a cartoon-sized bump on the back, like it's another head trying to grow, and Danny's hand is on my shoulder and she's trying to get me to lie back again on the fold-down zed-bed style arrangement.

~ Jesus Suzy, I thought you were dead, she says, and I remember the splash.

~ I thought you jumped, I say, and a sort of guilt comes over her.

~ Sorry Suzy, I figured it best to try and get away, but they got me further down. I didn't get far. Just as well they fished me out. Suzy, what are we going to do?

I sit up slowly, and my leg is numb and puffed and heavy and a huge throb in the centre of my back feels almost like a heel shape and the scar below it is also reliving its early days and pulsing like it has its own wee heart.

~ They put something on that. It looks pretty bad by the way, she says, and I carefully pull up the leg of the like tracky bottoms and there's a clean white dressing tight about the wound, and only a tiny spot of blood to indicate where the tear actually is.

~ That wee bastard thing. If it wasn't for that I might have—

I stop myself even trying to make an excuse. The lass caught me good and proper and more fool me for even squaring up. I should have realised after watching her demonstration at Magenta that she knows what she is doing, and there's no-one doesn't have a superior in any skill. I should just be grateful she spared me one of those kicks. But that may yet await me.

~ How long have I been out?

Danny instinctively flicks at the cuff of this like bright purple man's shirt to check her watch but it's gone and she raises empty palms.

~ They took everything, she says, and I kiss goodbye to the three-grand and more I had tight-rolled in the big elastic band.

I swing my legs across and try to stand up, but the leg won't allow it. I know movement is the best thing for it, but I'm so shagged out I probably couldn't move much anyway, and Danny urges me to lie back down.

~ Where are we then? seems the next natural question, but Danny's already shaking her head.

~ All I know is it took us about half an hour, maybe forty minutes to get here. It was a van, no windows. Motorway for the first twenty-five maybe, then very hilly and bendy and windy the rest of it. God only knows where we are, but I think it's like countryside, smelled like shite when we got out anyway. They tied my jacket round my head, and you were well out, but it was rough ground before getting in here. Maybe it's a farm or suchlike.

The room is small, and the old-style sash window has like fold-out carved interior storm-doors that have been fastened with two largish padlocks. There is an old fashioned fireplace with a hearth and grate, but the idea of doing a Santa is out of the proverbial, so that leaves the door. Danny must be reading my thoughts.

~ I've already tried it. Solid. And there's someone sitting outside it.

~ See any guns on the way, I ask, and she shakes the head again.

~ No tools at all, she says.

I find myself looking at the lampshade above, which, being flat on my back, is the natural point of focus, and it's like a toddler's thing, with silhouettes of like elephants and lions and such all chasing each other, and quite a jolly thing it is too. Then the wallpaper jumps into view as it also has like a paper border two-thirds up the wall going right round the room and it is similarly decorated with various exotic fauna, and I notice that the wallpaper itself is baby blue, and it sinks in that this is like a nursery we're in.

So this is someone's house, and maybe they have a baby, or the previous owners had one, and now the room is like a guest room doubling as a cell. Maybe it gets used as a sort of store-room, there being many cardboard boxes, some sealed, and one corner has a pile of old chairs stacked atop an old kitchen table, and there's a very nice old Welsh dresser against the wall by the door which is stacked with smaller boxes, as if someone's moved in and not got round to emptying and sorting their stuff. The circle of light on the ceiling has like ribbons of dusty spider-web swinging in whatever slight draught there is, and the place must have been lying empty for a while, but it feels a comfy wee room, almost happy, and given the situation we're in I can only attribute such a thought to the smell of childhood, 'cos that's what the out-of-place aroma is – it's baby talc, baby lotion, general baby-smell, fusty and distant but baby-smell right enough, and I do feel suitably helpless what with being bandaged and dressed in clothes not of my own, and like sent to bed in the strictest and most unwelcome way imaginable and very much confined to my room.

There's a chatter close to the door, and a key turns and a bolt slips and it's open and there's Penny B, all changed and dry as well, and looking a tad tired she is too but she manages a smile as she steps into the room and I don't know what sort of hate and rage must come over my face, and my breathing starts to quicken but I know she knows I'm in no position to start anything now.

She sits on the old-style chair near the well-filled

bookcase in the corner by the door and her two small stocky male colleagues stand nearer us, making like some human shield as it were. Danny shifts further up the bed, leaning against the wall with her arm curved round about my shoulders, her knees drawn up like she's resigned now and will take whatever's coming, but there is no vibe of imminent hassle, and this Penny waits for this other lass to enter, and she's carrying like a flask-type jug and a couple of plastic fluorescent beakers and she puts these down on the otherwise clear computer desk before she shuts the door.

~ How you feeling then ladies? asks Penny, and I stay silent, staring and wondering what it's all about.

~ You'll need a tetanus jag, she continues, so we'll get that sorted for you as soon as.

~ As soon as what? I say, and this Penny rubs her thighs and frowns and looks at the other lass before going on.

~ You know that one of your team is dead? she says, and Danny kind of tightens her hand on me and whimpers a bit. I nod.

~ Emma here can't go home. We only just made it away as it was. Lucky we saw you going through the crescent 'cos after getting on to the Kingsbridge Avenue the bridge was the one and only way you could get out again. Sorry if I hurt you, but from what I hear you're not the sort of character to start sparring with. I'm curious as to how good you really are, but that'll have to wait for another time what with your gammy leg and all.

~ Get on with it, I say, and she smiles.

~ It's a pity you didn't come out for a chat the other night. It might have saved all this. But you liaison officers are not exactly easy to get hold of what with being ex-directory and all. Maybe you think you're untouchable, is that it, or should I say, bulletproof?

There's an anger in her voice which makes it squeak as she ends her words, but I feel my own jaw clench and judder to ponder the sheer gall of her getting angry after what she did to Joanne, and she must see it 'cos she gets up and steps nearer the bed.

~ You're going to tell us the truth Suzy, or Francine, or whatever the fuck your real name is. You'll tell us the truth before you leave here. And don't worry. You will leave. You are free after all. This is a free country. You are free to go, but not until you tell us the truth, and that will take just a couple of hours.

So this lass Emma is pouring the stuff into the beakers, and Penny turns and takes the blue one from her and holds it out towards us.

~ Who's first then? she asks, and Danny holds me tighter and she's shaking, but from fear or rage I know not, and I haul myself up a bit more and I lean over and she passes the beaker and I look inside and it's milky tea.

~ What's in it? I ask, and Penny half-shrugs, standing back and letting Emma come forward with the red cup, and Danny accepts it with hand atremble as Emma explains.

~ Two young ladies such as yourselves must be familiar with Whammers. Well, this will have pretty much the same effect as a mild Whammer at first. After ten minutes you'll feel increased heart-rate and slight flushing, then heart-rate will slow to about sixty a minute and you'll calm and feel quite cold. Another ten minutes and you'll feel as if you're asleep. You'll be awake, of course, and you'll hear and see everything about you, but you'll feel very deeply relaxed and you'll be very sharp memory-wise. It's a bit like some folk get when they're hypnotised, but you're not in any sort of trance state, you'll be very wide awake and calm. And you'll tell the truth about anything you're asked, and you'll want to. Any questions?

She says 'any questions' with this like air-stewardess grinning voice, and Penny laughs aloud as do the two guys.

~ Come on then, says Penny, down the hatch, and I down mine in a one-er and toss the empty cup to Emma, which she clearly does not appreciate, and Danny takes a few gulps of hers and hesitates but I nod her to go on and she does.

~ Well, you've had your tea, so we'll go and get ours. See you in about half an hour ladies, says Penny, and they're up and off and the bolt slips and the key turns and I shift up against the wall to make room for Danny and she starts like bubbling again and I pull the thin feather quilt over to cover us both and the baby-smell is all about and for the first time since I can remember the words Hail and Mary come popping into my head so I take that as a hint from on high and start praying like fuck.

Emma clearly knows her stuff, 'cos although my sense of time seems to disappear, and I cannot truthfully say if it's ten minutes or two hours that pass what with the multitude of memories flitting through my head, but I get this like pure bloated feeling and it's like all my personal blood allowance has shifted into my head and my hands, and my fingers feel like they're the size of barrage balloons and someone's trying to stuff a three piece suite into my skull, and although I want to get up to let the blood drop out again, I can't move, and Danny's curled up into a pure ball with her knees almost touching her face and she's shivering but I'm as hot as a bit of toast and then I get shivery as one of Kelly's penguins and Danny holds onto me and we're both shaking and gob-chattering like half-drowned kittens. Then, very slowly, the blood starts to go back into the rest of me and I'm calm and still as is Danny, and it's like we've been sort of melted into the one person and our heartbeat is the same, and just as Emma predicted this beat is slow and loud and like a watch swinging to make us calmer and deeper with every beat. I'm sure I fall asleep, but when the bolt slips and the key turns and the door is opened it's as if my eyes are open and I can see every movement, every detail of the door and Penny and Emma and their two wee lads entering, and it's all right now. No anger, no confusion, no more worries.

So this other room they take me into is a very warm and comfy like library sort of lounge-type set-up, with many shelves bearing a multitude of books and files and papers and such, all quite neat and stacked in wee towers where they've had no space left on shelves, and there's two video monitors and sundry computer-related boxes and gear lying around but no actual telly as such, which seems a tad strange.

The ceiling is very high, and I get to have a right good look at that what with being flat on my back again and staring at this big ornate ceiling rose, and someone's gone to the bother of painting the different whorly leavey things in various shades of green and gold, and it's all very tasteful and has like a home-show sort of style about it what with the very long and heavy velveteen drapes across the bay-window and knobbly-kneed armchairs and a very posh-looking three seater dark red leather settee.

So I'm flat-out on this settee and the pain in my leg is still there but no more than maybe a mild leg headache sort of thing, and the bump on the back of my crust is still athrob but not a patch on what it was less than an hour back. I can open my eyes no problem, but it's nicer having them shut, and the smell of this room is not nearly as nice as was the nursery, it's more an adult's room with traces of fag smoke and booze and assorted other adulty smells, and I'm feeling pretty good about it all now, just as predicted. Although I can see what the lass Emma was on about when she said it was similar to a Whammer rush, I'm not seeing anything like the things I see then, and don't expect to either. There's a definite twingling in the guts right enough, but it's like the feeling you get after you've had a right good feed of your favourite scran and you're like ready for a kip but it's a nice time you're having so you're having to struggle slightly to stay awake so that you can enjoy more of it, like when you're wee on Christmas day and you got up dead early to open your presents so that mid-afternoon you start falling asleep on the carpet holding your toys, and Mum and Dad and sundry others are chatting and boozing and smoking and they just put a blanket over you rather than even try putting you to bed on this special day.

And it's like Mum's voice is asking me to wake up, although it's not that she's asking. She's asking how I like my job, and what my telephone number is, and what's my address and my full name, and what's the correct spelling of that. And then she's asking who my best pal is, and I'm talking about Joanne and her family and remembering our best days and sundry daft arguments and I'm crying as I describe her lying against the lamp-post with dark blood like a bib down her front.

Pretty soon I can't remember how many questions I've already answered, and I don't care. I've told the truth to every single one of them, and why shouldn't I given that I've done nothing wrong anyway. I'm not even angry about having to answer them. It's like I'm answering for my own good, which is kind of loopy I know, what with me being held prisoner and made to wear like teenagers' night-wear and generally being made a fool of. My body is very heavy and like asleep, but I feel as if I want to get outside and have a good run and jump and muck about. Maybe later.

~ Your national insurance code again please, says Emma, so I trot it out for the third time, and I can hear her pen making marks on the paper, and one of Penny's lads mutters something about the video-camera and I hear like a tape cassette being changed.

~ Who were you looking for tonight?

~ Penny, if that's her name. Her with the scar.

~ Why?

~ She killed my pal, I say, but very matter-of-fact I am, not callous, but straight down the line, no voice-quivering, no eyeball-tingling.

~ You're talking about Joanne Friel again?

~ Yes.

~ Would it surprise you to know that it wasn't Penny who killed her?

There's a slight ripple then of what I suppose must be

surprise right enough, so I answer accordingly, but still very calm and cool and soft of voice.

~ Yes, it would, I say.

~ But if it was the truth, then you would have to believe it, wouldn't you? she says, and I digest her question before I answer.

~ If it's the truth, I'll believe it, I say, and very much do I mean that given that I always was brought up to believe, and would like to think that I managed to reach the conclusion myself, that truth is what you believe, and even if it is not particularly beneficial or attractive or easy to understand, the truth can only be the truth if it is believed.

~ What if I told you that you killed her? says Emma then, and I don't know what she wants me to say, so I stay silent.

~ Do you believe you killed Joanne? asks Penny.

I open my eyes and the ceiling rose seems very large and near, and my mind is rewinding and slowing and freeze-framing, and then the search is over and I'm free to answer,

~ No I don't, I say.

As she rattles on through a series of questions regarding my wages and bosses' names and technical doings connected with the structure of the teams and management and suchlike, I'm pondering what she said about Penny not killing Joanne, and the suggestion that it may have been me. Of course, I didn't see it all, and have only the reports of Harry and Shuggs and Josie, but it strikes me now that none of them did actually finger her, none went on about the scar or described her gear and all that. And Shuggs did say he thought they were all guys. And I know it wasn't me. If it was, I would certainly be shocked, but the memory is clear and straightforward, and I realise that the fact they're even asking further confirms that they don't know either.

~ Who is D. Jones? comes the next question, but it's not from Emma, and I open my eyes to see that Penny has taken her place and in her hand is a small card which looks familiar. I feel a sudden panic, like I really want to, need to, answer her question and I should be able to, but I purely can't. I stammer, as if the explanation is on the tip of my tongue but won't come out, but I know I really don't have one. I feel small and miserable, as though I've failed.

~ I can't remember, I say, and Penny turns the card to face me and I recognise it and remember the grumbly-faced Miss Warnes at Spring Central that morning.

~ He's some guy I've to call if I need anything, I say, suddenly relieved and happy.

~ Have you ever met this man? she asks, and I shake my head.

~ Have you made any arrangements to meet him yet?

~ No.

~ Have you contacted him at all?

~ No.

Emma crouches down beside me and holds my wrist for a few seconds, then reaches across and another beaker of tea is in front of me and I don't even wait to be asked, just down the lot.

~ Francine, says Penny, and I look at her and I know I'm smiling and know I should hate myself for it but I can't. I just want to be nice, to co-operate, for everything to just stay exactly the way it is. She leans forward in the seat and she's smiling as well, and it makes the scar kind of split, makes it bend, and it's nice.

~ You remember me don't you? she says.

~ Yes. You were at Magenta the other night.

~ Before that Francine. You've seen me before that, haven't you? she says, and I'm about to shake my head but then don't.

~ Think, Francine. Remember.

I close my eyes, and it's like rewinding a video-tape only doing it like a thousand times faster than normal, and I'm on top of the horse statue in the George and the battle is well and truly under way and it slows, and I'm watching the thickest part of the crowd, hoping to catch a glimpse of Joanne and Bobby, and the first bottles have already been flung so the rozz have like lowered their heads in formation to make a dark line of round hat-tops and I focus on the flag-wavers directly in front of this line of rozz and there is Penny, down by the left hand side of the bus-stage thing, and she's wearing a white cotton sleeveless shirt and a sort of blueish flat cap and her back's turned to me cos she's giving it pure pelters at the rozz afront the hall, but she turns to beckon someone nearer and I close in and freeze-frame and it's her alright.

~ In the George, yes, I remember.

~ Has anyone approached you to give evidence at the inquiry into the George deaths? she asks, and I'm looking at her and the face in front of me keeps getting overlaid with the freeze-frame of her in the square that day, and it's like I'm seeing both at once but I can still hear and understand what she's asking.

~ No.

~ Did you know that you will be called? she asks then.

~ No, I say again, and I get a tingling where I know I should feel fear, only it's the absence of it that I'm aware of.

~ Francine, she says again, low and very calm, and I look at her and she's very close, almost off the chair, staring right into me.

~ Francine, I didn't kill Joanne. Do you believe me? she says, and my eyes are riveted on hers and for a few seconds I switch my gaze from one eye to the other, really staring into her pupils and she doesn't move, and eventually I make my mind up.

~ Yes. Yes, I do.

~ Do you want to help me get the people who did? she says then, and this time I don't hesitate,

~ Yes. Yes, I do.

It's impossible to even guess what time it is when the door of the nursery is opened again and Danny comes in looking as drained as I feel, and she slumps down on the wee bed beside me but the door's kept open and the smaller of the two like guards comes in and he's got a tray laden with bowls of steaming scran and he leaves it on the desk and walks back out, leaving the door open.

It must be the effect of the Whammeresque drink, but the pain in my leg has subdued somewhat and is now more of a specific throb, so I can trace my fingers over the dressing and locate the length of the tear, and it's not as bad as I feared earlier but a tetanus will still be needed. Free to go whenever we've told the truth. That's what she said.

Danny kind of peers out the open door as I drag a couple of old chairs from the stack atop the table in the corner and drag them over to the desk, and there's knives and forks there, metal too, so this mob obviously feel that we are no longer worthy of basic precautions, or else are indulging in some sort of social-worker type trust building exercise.

The grub is most welcome, and my stomach sort of spasms when the first forkful goes down. It's some kind of chunky soup, thick enough perhaps to be classable as a stew, laden with thick wedges of meatyish mushroom-tasting material, and heavy with garlic or somesuch other member of the onion family. Danny has her bowl wiped clean with the buttered bread in a couple of minutes, and is hungrily watching me as I do my best to catch up. I give her my bread, and this she wolfs in true Danny fast-breaking mode, probably wishing the bread was toasted and she had her usual pot of cheap strawberry jam-substitute to spread atop it.

She looks a tad worried as I quiz her on what happened during her interrogation.

~ Suzy, I said some things I don't know if I should have, she says, and she's examining the inside of the stew-bowl like hoping it might make like a magic porridge pot and refill at her whim, and I half-wonder if the stuff has even worn off yet right enough, 'cos I'm still not getting any anger back, and truth be told, feel quite flat and calm and can't be bothered thinking up escape plans and suchlike.

~ Like what? I ask, and she gives me a quick glance and there's wetness again there in the big brown Danny-peepers.

~ I said I wanted to have your job, you know, like they were asking if there was any tension between us and I was like, well, yeah, we had a fight the other night, only

I made sure I told them what it was about and all that.

~ And do you want it? I ask then, and she looks up again, surprised and perhaps just a tad scared, not knowing perhaps how gloopy and laid-back I am now.

~ It doesn't have to be your job, you know, I just like to think I might be able to do it, you know, have my own team and all that.

I feel a sudden deep sadness for dear big Danny. As coarse and daft as she sometimes is, she only wants to get some dosh and have a boyfriend and go on holidays to sunny places and save up for a car or whatever, and she's not a bad lass, not deep down.

~ You can have it then, I say before taking a long swig of the milk.

She stares with big Danny-gob slowly opening, and a frown develops like she's trying to work out if she's heard right.

~ I'm not joking. You can do it, and I don't want it anymore, so when this is all done and dusted I'll send in a recommendation along with my resignation appli-cation and if you do what they tell you there's no reason why you can't. You did the course, they've already spent a lot of dosh on training you, and we've been in the top five Western teams for the last three months solid. Sure, why not.

~ Why you chucking it? she asks, but there's an unmissable excitement in her voice.

~ See when they were doing that stuff, all those ques-tions, there was only one I couldn't answer. You know how easy it was answering, I could have lay there all night and kept going, but just the once I was stumped, and I still don't have an answer.

For a half-second I check myself, wondering why I'm

telling Danny all this. My style of leadership, and maybe even the predominant feature of my fighting style, is not to give anything away, to conceal weakness and indecision by concealing everything. Much as I can say hand on heart, and probably did last night, that I love Danny and Kelly and dear departed Gerry, I don't exactly show it all that well, but that's maybe been 'cos of the job.

~ She asked me why, I say, and Danny grimaces while raising her face and draining the cup of the last of her milk.

~ Why what? she says, a big drip of creamy milk running down her chin and being chased by her tongue-tip.

~ Why do it? They asked me if it was the money, and I said no, and they asked me if it was the violence, and that was another no, or maybe the excitement, not that either. They want to know what I'm doing working for the Commissioner's Office, and I keep just telling them it's a job, but that doesn't seem to be enough for them so they ask all these myriad wee questions like as if they're trying to catch me out or something but I'm being straight with them all the way. I don't know why I'm doing it. I really don't. I can't tell them the truth of why I'm doing it 'cos there is no truth, there is no reason. So, I'm not doing it any more. That's it.

~ You honestly think I could do it? she says then, happy.

~ I'm sure you could, I say, but if you do, make sure you know why you're doing it, 'cos this is doing my head in. I wish I'd listened to Joanne. Jesus, I could have been working in the poxy library, and if I would have stayed with her this might never have happened at all. Now poor Gerry as well. And it's my fault.

If filling-up is a sign of the stuff wearing off then wearing off it must be, 'cos I fill up right enough and put my head down on top of folded arms and it's not like I'm sobbing, 'cos suddenly I haven't even the energy for that. It's as if it's all I can do just to breathe and let the tears well and drop as they will, and I get back on the wee zed-bed and curl up into myself and try to wish the thoughts and the guilt away and pray to be left alone to sleep.

When I wake it's Emma shaking my arm, and the instant my eyes are open I know whatever they gave me has worn off 'cos the madness is back and them giving me the gloopy truth-drink only adds to the fury. I snarl and turn and am up in two seconds, and she's backed off to the door, palms aloft surrender-wise, but with her two like bodyguards right close by, and I don't care much about that anyroad and am about to take them on when Penny B appears behind and they part for her and she's through and only feet away and the wetness of the bridge comes back to me, and the speed of her and being breathless without even seeing it coming, and the sensible part of me holds it all in and listens to her.

~ It's alright, Francine, she says, and that's like another red rag.

~ Suzy to you, bitch, I say, and very growly too, like I'm possessed by some dog-like creature.

She smiles and waves back the others, who retreat beyond the doorway, and I'm aware of the bulky shape of Danny out there. Penny nears.

~ Bit of Jekyll and Hyde aren't we, Suzy? Maybe you

should drink tea more often. There's someone here you might want to talk to, she says, and I'm sure she would love to hit me again, and must know how much I want to hit her, but I can't fancy my chances at all. Bide my time.

~ Who would that be then? I ask, and back off, lowering my arms.

~ Bob! she shouts, and then he's there in the doorway, small and red-eyed and very puppyish and lost looking.

~ They got you too? I say, sort of thinking out loud, but he doesn't say anything.

~ Bob has something to tell you, so I'll leave you alone for a bit. By the way, Jim will be here in about half an hour, so we'll get you that tetanus shot before we leave.

~ We? I say, and the smile has gone and she looks a tad tired of explaining and being nice, and she backs off and out and Bobby is in with us and the door is slammed, bolt slips, key turns.

Bobby is rigid and white, and maybe he fears I'll vent it all on him, but I'm spent again, leg throbbing like jiminy, so a quick hobble back to the sack and I sit, leaning against the wall, pull the covers over my legs. He sits at the desk thing with Danny and starts rabbitting and greeting in equal measure.

~ It's my fault, he gushes, and Danny gives him a wad of like bog-roll and he blasts his beak into that.

~ You know these people? I ask, and he nods and rabbits on, and for the very first time it feels like I'm getting answers instead of more confusion, and from the sporadic sobbing and inability to speak it is plain that young Bobby and Joanne must have been very much more of an item than I'd ever realised, and genuinely heartbroken is how he seems now.

~ I never meant for her to get into it, but she was interested. It's not like we're fucking terrorists man, you know? I was just into the camp, you know, up at the end of the park, and it was just like a laugh, good laugh and that, good crack, no hassle. It was after the George, mind that day? After that man, all sorts of shit starts happening. We're all out on bail and that, but what the fuck are they going to do eh, bang us all up and say it was our fault? If those rozz wasn't inside the Hall there wouldn't have been any crush at all, everyone would just have piled in and had a party. So what? But then Penny's flat gets done good style and she can't go back, all her stuff's gone, all her files and that. Like, she's into it big-style, loads of contacts down South and that, but there's no way she's like some mad unabomber or something. That's when Joanne gets the start in the library mind? And you know what she's like with the computers and that, so she comes up to mine this day and she's got like this printout she got from the work, and this is heavy stuff, it's like internal rozz stuff and she's got in there, like hacked into it, and there's names and addresses, and Penny's on it, and Emma, and this breakdown of who's at the camp and what they're claiming benefits–wise and they've all got this rating, like some kind of score. And my name's on it as well, and where I sign, and my Mum and Dad's address, right, so I'm pure like that, panic-stations, and we show it to Penny the next night, and she's like going mental, over the moon, really freaking, and she's all over Joanne like she's the answer to all her prayers, and it's all this can-she-get-more, is-it-hard-to-access and all that, so Joanne tries with the set-up in here, but 'cos we're not on the same council lines, she can't get into it, so she has to do it from work but she says she will, and that's her well-in with Penny. She gets more, almost every day she comes back with something else, and she says like no-one bothers their shirt 'cos she's on the flexi-time and she can go in pretty much anytime she wants, so she always stays a bit later and the rest of them are offsky and she can blast into this stuff and you know what she was like anyway, she loves it.

He breaks out a packet of tobacco and rolls a fag and Danny makes one as well and I get her to make one for me, not being adept at the manipulation of small pieces of gummed paper. Bobby has got it together a wee bit, and it's like he's been rehearsing it all in his head and expected to have to say all this stuff at some point.

~ So we all get lifted just before Christmas, there's hardly any of us left in the camp then with it being so cold and wet, and they want to get the workies in to level the space so they kind of catch us unawares and in they come team-handed and lift the lot of us, and Joanne's there that day with me, so they take us down Central and it's all this stuff about charges and Joanne will have to lose her job and such what with her being a council worker and all that, and they let me out next day but Joanne's kept in. We've got the same lawyer, and I'm like on to him non-stop about it and he's pure rubber-earing me and giving it all this shite about complications in Joanne's case and she's helping with enquiries and such, but it's like three days she's kept in, and when she comes up to mine on the Tuesday she's a pure state and won't tell me what happened and all that, but she wants to see Penny right away and she's like really bottling it. So I call Emma and tell her and she picks us up and we stay here the night and Joanne fills in Penny. Turns out that the rozz knew their stuff was being hacked and downloaded, but it took them ages to trace it 'cos Joanne had covered it up really well but they got some super expert type in and he managed to pinpoint it to the library, but it wasn't till she got lifted with me at the camp that they put two and two together, so they've put the fear of God into her and she'll be going to jail for sure unless she co-operates with them and even then it's not guaranteed that they'll manage to keep her out of the poky, it's only if she comes up with good stuff that they'll try and get immunity, and what they want is for Joanne to just carry-on like normal and be a spy, real cloak and dagger double-cross stuff. But that's Penny over the moon yet again 'cos Joanne's told her, and it's like the big breakthrough as far as she's concerned. So we just went on as normal, and Joanne was like blagging into the rozz files as she was before, and getting all this bumph which was loaded with rubbish and we knew it, and she was getting visits every Friday evening from these two guys and she would give them a pile of shite about what was happening, and bits of it were true but it was all harmless stuff, like where the parties were on that weekend, any new folk she'd seen knocking about that week, all that sort of stuff, and they'd take all that away, but it would never show up on the stuff she was blagging so it looked like they didn't know she was still with us.

Joanne working for the rozzloiderlings? If it wasn't Bobby telling me this I would laugh and forget it as some joke of rather sick variety. But it starts to make sense now why she wasn't getting in touch, what with me being in the Commissioner's Office, and therefore a sworn enemy of these idealistic anti-road types.

But knowing Joanne, and even with all of this coming as something of a surprise, I still think I knew her better than most, and I'm sure she must have been happy then to know that she was even trying to do something right, something that she thought might make a difference, even if she was pissing in the wind.

But what took her to Magenta that night? I still don't know who stuck the knife in her, who left her dying there.

The suspects have been dropping off like onion skins, and it tires and pains me to think how many more may still have to be unpeeled. But seeing Bobby now, and knowing how much he must hurt and knowing that he must know how much I'm hurting also, it's like there's even more reason now to find out who and why.

I ask Bobby about the funeral, but it turns out that her body is not being released for burial until sundry examinations have been carried out, and only her Mum has been allowed to see her for eye-dee purposes. He hasn't been to see her folks, but called them, and her Dad answered and asked him who the fuck he was, which sounds most unlike preacher-language, but understandable.

Bolt slips, key turns, door swings open and it's Emma and Penny and their little guards, and Penny hands me a mobile phone and the card given to me by the grumpy Miss Warnes, and there is the name of D. Jones scrawled on the back with his mobile number and looks like I have not much by way of choice now and I listen to Penny's instructions.

It's all very clear what she wants, and she's calm and talks to me straight in the eye and level, and I hold her eyes as she speaks and despite the suspicions I still have,

I know that I do trust her, so she gets the gear ready at the wee computer table and everyone kind of settles down and then we're all set and she tells me to just do it in my own time and I'm focussed and keen and ready and nod and punch in the numbers and I know I'm just a small part of it all now, but that's fine.

CHAPTER TWELVE

The dialling tone is like a human impersonation of a dialling tone, a soft baby-dinosaur noise. There's a bit of feedback from the wee monitor that Penny has which allows all to hear the conversation, so she fiddles with a knob and the shrill throb stabilises then fades. The woman who eventually answers repeats the last six digits of the number I dialled and asks which name I require.

~ Mr Jones please. Mr D. Jones.

~ And your name please? says the woman.

Maybe it's like residual whammeresque drink effect, but I pause and have to make my mind up. Suzy? Francine?

~ Suzy, I say then, Suzy Brallahan.

There's a very long pause full of clicking and a very dodgy electronic rendition of like Home on the Range or somesuch similarly plodding twangly country and western type dirge, and then it's a tinny contact and the voice of this man is very smiley and kind, like your favourite uncle, and it's as if I've got him half-way through humming some tune and he carries on humming snatches of it as he checks something.

~ Suzy, ah, yes, now, would that be Francine? Ah, I see, right, that's that, I see, that's why I had the two names there, sorry about that. Now then, eh Suzy, should I call you Suzy? Fine, right then. Suzy, I was talking to your lawyer yesterday and I was told to expect you to call so, ehm, how can I help?

He stops dead then, not humming any more, and Penny is nodding and urging me, pointing at her watch.

~ I have to meet, I say, and the pause only stops when he sort of hums in such a way that he obviously wants me to tell him why.

~ I don't know what to do any more, I say in sad lost puppy mode, I can't go back home and I'm hurt but I can't even go to the hospital. Miss Warnes said I was to call you if I was in any bother. Well, I am.

~ You're hurt? he says, and sounds aghast, as if he's known me all his life.

~ Look, I can't talk now, I've got to go, I say, and he sort of panics then, talks very fast and kind of harsh teachery mode.

~ Where are you? he says, and it's like a demand.

~ I'm not sure, I say, and the smile has definitely gone from his voice now and I make like quick rasping sniff noises and breathless gasps like I'm in real pain and knackered.

~ Tell me where you are.

With my inferior peeper quality I'm having to sort of squint at the paper with the instructions so Penny slides it closer to me and the letters blur then sharpen.

~ I don't know the name of the road. It's at the back of the cemetery, I can see the big cigarette factory.

~ Mills? he says, and quite excited he is now.

~ Yeah, that's it I think.

~ Are you alone?

~ What? I say, and Penny holds this other wee phone up beside me and the line starts coming over all mad static.

~ Go to the factory gates, he says.

~ I can't. I'm getting followed.

~ Who's following you? he shouts, and Penny brings the phone nearer and then takes the mobile from me and clicks it off.

~ Fine. That'll let him stew. Well done, Suzy. Let's go next door. I'll show you what we've got on this character. It's as well you know the type of person you're up against.

So we all plod into the lounge where the computer is glowing green and Emma calls up this file and there's a like totally blurred picture of a face which is like the grainy style of a tiny snippet of video or telly but magnified many times, and it's such a bad picture that you'd be as well not having any picture at all really, but this face belongs to D Jones, who is also D Smith, and there's the list of all his other names and it's like he's got this whole alphabet of first names, from Alan right to Zeth, but just Smith and Jones as surnames, and Penny lets me sit right next to Emma 'cos what with my eyesight I'm finding it hard out make out the writing, but I sit pretty much in total silence as Emma scrolls through the bumph they have on this guy, and it's like something out of a James Bond film, all the stuff he's done, the places he's been. He was in a unit of the army that's something like the SAS but just takes to do with domestic stuff, but he's like one of their pure main men and is very adept at planning ways of trapping terrorists and other undesirables. So he's been in as a sort of consultant with the Commissioner's Office since before anyone even knew it was going to happen, and his Operation Control section of it is the bit where they gather all the information on the staff and possible internal trouble and suchlike.

Turns out that Joanne managed to get this after she hacked into the Edinburgh Central Office of the Commissioner's Office, and Emma explains that there's like almost a thousand pages of this stuff, and I'm in there, all the Liaison Officers for the whole country are in there with detailed breakdowns of our abilities and weaknesses, family background, you name it.

I ask Emma if I can see what they've got on me and she asks Penny, and it's okay so up it comes and there's a photo of me that must've been taken from the Cherry basket with me and my little ladies, and the background stuff goes on for three pages and is all about me being a depressive character with high IQ and greatly unsettled family background and very violent and all that, but unlikely to be a source of any serious trouble on the basis that I have no apparent interest in political activity and have never been a member of any party and all that, and it's like quite shattering to see yourself described and analysed in this way and I eventually say enough.

So, it was this character Smithjones who was in charge of getting all this stuff on me, and it would have been his boys who followed me, took photos, compiled all this bumph. There's stuff on Danny and Kelly and

Gerry, and this amazes me somewhat given that Gerry, being a probation-hopper and all, was never taken in even though they knew her whereabouts, and this in itself is proof of serious rozz involvement given that all Liaison Officer applicants are closely rozz-vetted before even being allowed on the course.

And it takes maybe an hour or something, but I sit and listen and look and Penny and Emma set it all out for me. The She Shaws was the cover they used for their organisation, which was only ever about stopping the new motorway to the South West, but the longer they went on the more covert stuff was being used against them, and they know now, thanks to all the stuff Joanne managed to get, that the She Shaws will be blamed for the George riot and punished accordingly to save the jobs of the top boys in the rozz, the council, the Commissioner's Office, the Press, and just about every-where and everyone else that had ever had anything to do with the scheme.

When Penny and the assembled Shaws came to Magenta the other night, they were looking for me, and they would have killed me, believing that I had somehow betrayed Joanne. It is so weird to hear anyone else talk about her, as Penny and Emma now do, with feeling, filling-up and getting angry. I suppose I never really thought about her being anyone else's friend, and the selfishness of that makes me feel small and ashamed.

Now that they spell it out, I can see it making some kind of sense, and it dawns that I am in as much trouble as they are seeing as how I am now forced to take sides, and what alternative do I have but to stick with these girls, the only ones who have made any kind of effort to show me the truth. And for all that I don't give a Donald about their politics or their idealism or whatever else that may motivate them, it seems now that we have a common enemy, and I know I'm getting closer to who killed Joanne, and closer to a fight I'm not fit for.

When we get outside I'm blinded by the strength of the light. The sky is as blue as blue can be, and there's not a single cloud anywhere.

Danny was almost right about it being a farm, there being many open fields about which are all turned over and deep reddy brown with multitudes of white and black birds walking in the furrows and partaking of the worms or whatever it is they find in there, and the fields are edged with great tall trees that are still, but leaves of gold and scarlet and every colour in between are dropping off and like floating into the edges of the fields and sundry cows and sheep can be seen here and there, eating grass and looking about and generally quite happy with their lot.

It's a cold day, and everything looks very bright and clean after the mad rain last night, and the colours are so sharp they hurt my peepers and I have to squint as we wait for someone or other, and a couple of the guys are having a smoke and Danny is at it again after her being off the smokes for ages, so I get her to roll me one as well. I watch her as she fiddles with the paper, and the bruise on her face is violet and crimson and will spread a lot further. My own wounds sort of pulse in sympathy, and I get like a view of us as if from above and we are a rather sorry sight it has to be said, what with the dark boiler suits we've been given not fitting too well at all, and the woolly bunnets are not at all cutting-edge chic and very scratchy into the bargain.

We sit on this low stone wall. There's light frost on the muddy ground which has like hardened with footprints intact, and we rub our hands together and puff and wait. The smoke from the fags hardly moves in the air, and the only sounds are of birds tweetering and shirping, and now and then a sheep shouts to another one. All in all it's pretty much a perfect place, apart from the smell of like raw effluent which hangs about, and I'd be very happy to stay here for a while and forget all the heaviness and hassle.

Back into the van which brought us here, though I recall nothing of the first journey, and pretty soon we're on the motorway and making it speedy for town. Wee Bobby drives, Penny and Emma in the passenger seats. Me and Danny and the two wee guys are in the back, propped against the walls, and Penny tells us to keep right down, and it's shades of last night, only I can't believe that that was only a few hours ago and not days, as it certainly seems. Penny lets me use her phone after I assure her I'm only calling my Mum, and when Mum answers she's in one of her like pure hyper neurotic moods, all finicky and panicky and generally ahop with excitement, and I have to let her gibber.

~ That phone hasn't stopped, she says, all night it was going, and every time I picked it up I was thinking it must be you and all I get is this mad buzz like you're trying to get through. Didn't get a wink of sleep the both of us, worried sick. And then there's a man up this morning.

~ Did he say his name? I ask, and I tug at Penny's jacket to get her attention.

~ Mr Smith. David Smith. Nice wee man, he got your

machine fixed, only took him about half an hour and that was him, but he says any more bother you've to call him and he'll get it sorted. He says that's why the phone wasn't working either, 'cos the computer's the same line as the phone and all that, and he's right enough 'cos that's the phone working alright now.

~ Mum, this guy, was he alone? I ask, and Mum hums and haws and I hear her covering the phone and shouting through to her man.

~ Well, there was another two pals with him but he just did the job himself and they were outside. Guy saw them in the corridor when he came back up from the shops. I did offer if they wanted a cuppa but he said they were so busy but thanks all the same and that. Seems a very nice lad though. Do you work with him dear?

~ Sort-of, Mum, yeah. Look, if he calls, or anyone else, I'm on my way home right. Don't know when I'll be back, maybe about an hour or so, right? Right?

~ Okay dear, she says, and I click off and Penny's darkened face is awaiting an explanation.

~ Someone was in my flat this morning fucking about with the computer. I wasn't expecting anyone up and there's nothing wrong with it that I know of. Think it might be that guy?

Penny scans me very carefully, as if looking for signs of lying, but then she nods and lets out a wee moan of like wondering.

~ Yeah. Might well be.

Coming into the Spring from the South seems a bit strange, especially in daylight, and the buildings seem unfamiliar until I spot the brewery pipes, and can work things out from there. Being on the other side of the brewery-path, which we so seldom cross, I don't really know the landscape, and certainly not the ins and outs of the place as I do Viewhill, but me and dearest Danny certainly know it a lot better than Emma and Penny and her lads, that's for sure, and they listen carefully to our directions until we get to the back end of the cemetery by the hospital road, and that's where the van stops and Penny's boys get out and start hoofing it down towards the Boulevard, where the cigarette factory is.

Then it's up and around the hospital very slow, watching very carefully for any bods who might possibly be Mr Smithjones, and there's a few folk about with it being just gone half-eight, heading for their work or else finished their night shifts and making the plod home. The road winds up and about the hospital, then parallel with the motorway for a bit, and turns back down towards the cemetery, where there's a small like maze of old streets with big black-stoned houses, and it's here that Penny orders the van stopped. We're at the top of a very steep hill, houses on both sides, but there's a great view down the side of the cemetery, the back of the hospital, and the central part of the Boulevard including the front gates of the cigarette factory.

The figures of folk down on the Boulevard are dead wee, but Danny helps me identify the lads, and then I can see them making their way along the pavement running by the cemetery wall on the opposite side of the road from the factory. Buses are in abundance, this being the rush hour, and many children are being hurried along to school. There is a group of workies along at the traffic lights, almost out of sight, and they're taking up part of the road with pneumatic drills and a right racket it is too, even at this distance. There's guys just along from them who look like their bosses, hard hats and clipboards, the gaffers. The taxi-rank which serves the back of the hospital has five cars sitting on it, and the drivers are standing chatting in the sun.

But if Mr Jones is sitting in a car, as seems most likely, there's no chance of seeing him. Cars are parked along every inch of the road we've just followed round the hospital, and even on the Boulevard, which is supposed to be a no-park zone at rush hours, there's maybe two dozen in sight, likely belonging to parents who then walk their kids to the wee school down behind the factory.

The lads call from the factory gates to say that they're in place and check we have them in sight, and Penny calls back to confirm before passing the phone to me again. It's an old grave-house we're on top of, and it's like half-built into the side of the hill and we're peeking over the edge. This time I do feel a tad nervous given what I know about Mr Smithjones, but I can't deny there's an excitement there as well as I punch in the numbers and it clicks and buzzes and is picked up on three.

~ Hello, comes the voice, cheery and smiley as before.

~ Mr Jones, it's Suzy.

~ Suzy! I've been waiting. Problems with your phone I take it.

~ Sorry, it packed in on me. I should have gave you my number.

~ Ah, not to worry. You're alright?

~ Yes.

~ Now, give me a location before we lose you again.

~ I'm at the cemetery.

A movement by Penny, and she's pointing and Emma is following the line of her finger, and I shimmy a bit further up the verge to get a better view and there's the guys with the clipboards and one of them has a phone to his ear right enough and the other guys are standing silent, watching him.

~ Fine. Now, tell me where exactly, he says, and you can see him sort of staring up at the cemetery hill on our left, and it's like he's hoping to catch sight of me already, and the other two are also holding palms up to shield their eyes from the bright morning sun which must be reflecting off the headstones and old stone monuments.

~ Just at the top of the hill, the side facing the hospital. There's a like crypt thing, like a wee house, it's got Wilson over the door.

~ Right, he says then, I'm on my way. Just stay right where you are.

So this hard-hatted character starts walking right enough, and the two taller guys follow suit and they sort of trot across the road, obviously keen to get on with whatever it is they have in mind, and I call the number again and he's halfway over the waist-high wall that runs the length of the cemetery and he answers it as soon as he lands.

~ It's me again, I say, and he's still walking fast and talking, his colleagues ahead and mighty keen they are now, peering about like they're on some against-the-clock type competition, and they're getting clearer and closer at an alarming rate.

~ Just you, I say, your pals can stay by the road.

He clicks the phone off, punches in some other number and starts giving it gab to someone else.

Penny's lads have slipped over the wall and don't seem to have been spotted yet as they juke along behind the larger headstones, peeking out and sprinting, hiding again, and it's like one of these video games where you have to try and shoot them in the split second they appear, but they're going well and catching up with Mr Smithjones and cronies who by now have managed to get the bright yellow jackets off and they chuck them but keep the hard hats on.

Penny grabs my arm and I'm not well-pleased by this and turn sharpish and rather mowly I am too but she strengthens her grip and it's really quite sore and I know she wants my attention.

~ Don't fuck this up, Suzy, she sort of snarls, and there's like a thin line of very dense and creamy froth on her lower lip and most beastly it looks too on her what with the big scar down her face like pure white but red about the edges of it, like it's really throbbing and sore 'cos of the cold, and the general madness of her eyes, wide and grey and angry as angry can be.

I get down off the wee grave-house roof and onto the gravelly path. Maybe it's just like the accumulated frustration of wanting now for days to have someone to take it out on, but this Smithjones character seems to be a perfect candidate. Right now the possibility of him perhaps being involved in Joanne's murder doesn't matter 'cos everyone I've blamed so far had nothing to do with it, but as enraged as I now am, the ankle pain and back pain are swamped with numbing adrenalin and I know I'm making grunty high-pitched like moans of pure animal warning shots, and the stocky wee bastard just keeps coming up the steeper slope here near the top and I can hardly wait.

His boys are close with him now, and I stride to the brow of the hill with the gravel like crunching underfoot and then they see me, this is them maybe fifty yards away and then there's this silvery glint in the sunlight above their heads and this like urn thing for holding flowers, it comes down just in front of Smithjones and you can see he gets a bastard of a fright what with it just missing his noggin and cracking most loudly on the headstone just in front of him and breaking and spinning into its component parts, and his boys stop and whirl and then catch a glimpse of Penny's lads and go into their jackets and now we know they're gunned up. Smithjones resumes walking, like trying to make out he thinks I haven't seen him, and he's all smiles and open palms.

~ Suzy. At last! and he's making out he's out of breath and like knackered as he gets nearer and I can see now he's a small chap, probably just an inch or two on me, but certainly on the stocky and solid side of things physique-wise with big barrel-chest and the suit jacket looks quite tight about the shoulders and neck.

His lads are out of sight now, hidden behind separated stones and they're shouting some sort of instructions to each other and Smithjones is twenty feet away.

~ Thank God you're alright, he says, but the voice is the angry one without the smile, even though he's still smiling, and I pick up my stride pronto and when he sticks his right in under his armpit I know he's going for it so forward fast and in low at his legs just as he pulls the thing away and I'm still on the deck when he lands facing away but the gun is there right enough, dull metal and a right fat ugly wee thing it is too, so I have to be across his back fast and pin the arm down and a bit of digging and climbing and he squeals a couple of times with my heels juddering down his calves, and I bring up my left elbow very snappy and much pain surely when it lands right on that wee soft bit at the base of your neck and his hair is like very thin and smooth between my fingers as I twist his face towards me, then fold my palm quickly down his face, fingers grasping at his chin, and let his face push away just so much that index finger and middle finger catch a nostril each and scrunch down my thumb into his bristly cheek to secure the grip, and I'm fighting the urge to tear up hard and send the nose-splinters firing into brain-meat and I've well and truly got him and he knows it.

Emma is there and she stamps a couple of times on Smithjones's wrist, and the gun jumps away and Penny gets it, and I'm aware of Danny pounding past then, no doubt rushing to the aid of Penny's lads and Penny herself is down beside me and my arm is shaking as I strain not to pull, and he's making like really high pig noises and the snot is making my fingers slippy but no way I'm letting go and I keep his head tight in the crook of my arm and his hands are raised, every finger straining to get away from its neighbour. Penny squats in front of us and points the gun at his face and kind of nods at me so I release his nose and he makes a noise like a dog sneezing and wrinkles his beak most briskly and holds it and rubs it as the tears stream down his white face.

~ Get up, says Penny, but he sort of snorts again and I can't actually see his face but his expression has a most adverse effect on Miss Penny, and she goes very berserk and stands up before like kicking him very full-on and painful-sounding right in the middle of his face and the force of the kick knocks him flying back and of course me also, and a great howl comes out of him as I pull away from him and get up and back off with a pain of like paralysing intensity shooting down my back, and he's curled like a baby still inside the mother, but Penny's there again and another stamp, like she's a wee kid having a tantrum, and it's bang, yet another heel-stamp right on his ear this time and he curls even tighter and smaller, one hand atop his crust and the other between his legs.

Penny takes a sudden interest in the fate of the others, and climbs atop the very nearest substantial stone to get a better viewpoint, and Emma bolts downhill and ducks down behind a granite slab, peeking out with the gun pointing skyward and very professional looking too, but there's no-one to be seen, and I guess they're all hiding behind stones and wondering who'll make the next move, and the shouts are like echoing and bouncing and sound much further away than they probably are.

Smithjones rolls over, gets to his knees and looks up at me. It's hard not to feel sorry for him what with his nose properly mashed and great long swinging strings of blood and mucus making this like alien glue-creature at the end of his beak and if this was twelve at night up the town or on the brewery-path you would have this guy down as a drunk who got waylaid by nerrdowells. His arms drop and he kind of sways back and forth like he's ready to keel over but manages to stay upright in a very wobbly and like inebriated manner, and his eyes have glazed like he's dreaming about something nice.

Seeing this gore in fresh morning light is quite sick-making I should say, and he sort of feels at his mouth, checking his dental arrangement, and he's getting kind of smiley again as he gets back to his feet and then, with a high like squeal he turns very swift of foot towards where Penny is on tiptoe on the stone, and I shout to her as he gets nearer, and there's two cracks of like car back-firing as she turns and kicks again but this one doesn't connect and she lands most awkwardly on the other side of the waist-high stone, and Jones sees his chance and goes launching his body like rugby-style right over the stone onto Penny, and very cat-fightish it looks by the time I get there and they're rolling over and over and he looks mighty strong does this chappie as Penny no doubt has noticed.

They roll until another headstone stops them, and it happens that Penny is on top but he's a good grip on her throat and is sort of hauling her face nearer his but she's pounding away good style at his neck and then she grips it hard and I can see she's pushing her fingers hard up under his voice box, and he's trying the same on her, and maybe it's just a matter of who starts it first will win, or maybe who can keep the most breath in, but he goes limp first, and as soon as his hands fall away from her neck Penny punches him another cracker on the side of his face before jumping up and taking several mega breaths and massaging her neck in a mildly panicky manner.

For a relatively small chappie he's certainly heavy enough, and we have to wait for Danny to help us get him up the slope and into the grave-house with Wilson over the door which is concealed behind a great many large rhododendron-type bushes and in we get and there is much puffing and wheezing all round. Penny tells me to stay watch him, which I'm very happy to do, and off she goes with Emma. I drag Smithjones into the damp corner of the wee room, which is like a totally festering hole full of empty cider bottles and sundry other litter and bits of old wet clothes and this single mattress covered in moss and the smell of piss and filth is extremely boak-making. He sorts of grunts and whistles, like he's snoring, but it's likely that his windpipe's crushed so I kind of prop him up and loosen his collar and pump at his chest for a bit until the noise lessens. Smithjones can't be allowed to die just yet. A shift and shuffle and I get up and about fast and there's Penny filling the low thin doorway.

~ The van's gone, she says, and then she pauses and listens and I get to the doorway and she raises a finger to closed mouth and I stop and then the sound comes, the sirens, maybe from away over at Spring Central, but also from other parts, and Emma appears, breathless, with Smithjones' gun, and there's a shot from downhill, then another, and we pile inside to find that Smithjones has got onto his knees and is crawling towards us. I kick him back towards the corner. Emma goes through his pockets, gets the phone, gives it to Penny. A 'copter approaches overhead, and we're looking at each other and it's like we know it's all over.

His phone bleeps, Penny answers and listens.

~ We've got your man here, she says, then listens again and slumps into a crouch just by the doorway when whoever it is rings off.

~ Emma, she says very weak and like resigned, and her friend crouches beside her.

~ Listen, Suzy, if you want to make a bid for it, go now. We're fucked, says Penny, and very poorly she looks now.

I ponder my options now. Not a lot. Those shots down the hill could only have come from Smithjones' lads, and there will already be more of them coming up the hill on all sides. There's no way out.

I squat beside Smithjones who's croaking in wee short breaths and very bloated of face. I shift across to face him, and even with it being extremely gloomy I can see that he's looking at me.

~ I'm not going anywhere, I say, and I'm not looking at the girls but I can hear one of them crying like very panicky and girly.

~ Who killed Joanne? I say quietly, and his eyes don't leave mine.

~ Fuck you, he says, and he actually manages a smile.

I feel so calm and so peaceful, it's like I've taken a new delivery of mercury on board, and I won't kill him right now, but I turn to the girls and it's Penny who's crying, hands over face, and I extend an open hand to Emma.

~ Give me that, I say, and she lowers her eyes cautious-style and grips the weapon tighter, aiming it in my general direction.

~ It's either that or bare hands, I say, and she looks down at Penny.

Penny is spent. Her eyes are closing, and it's the first time I've noticed the blood. It's shining dark on the surface of her boiler-suit, oozing between her fingers where she's got her right breast clasped.

~ It's over, Suzy, Emma says as I move closer, hand still open and waiting.

~ I have to know, I say, and Penny's eyes are like staring through me and she's still breathing but you can see she's on the way out, and Emma holds out the wee stumpy gun and turns to her pal and tries to lie her down and I'm over at Smithjones again and I've never even held a gun before and don't know if it'll work or not but I press the end of it right into the fucker's forehead and hold his throat with other hand.

~ Tell me who killed Joanne Friel, I say, and he's gazing right into me and there's no fear in him.

~ Official truth, it was you. Off the record, it was Robert. Robert Harris. Satisfied?

I scream, pull the trigger, and nothing happens.

CHAPTER THIRTEEN

Five years is a long time inside when you're eighteen, and most fortunate I am that I managed to control my temper and keep a clean slate for the half-time rule to be applicable. If there wasn't still so much bad feeling against me I'd be back in Magenta, but the Pinks and sundry other Maggie and Cherry residents chipped in to open a contract on me, and I've heard it's about twenty-five grand and still gaining interest, so I guess I'll stay put. I've never been mad on the English, but I'm getting used to it and can even pass for a Brummie when I put my mind to it, and that's only three years here.

Anyway, it could be worse. Thank Good God Almighty I couldn't figure out how to work that gun otherwise I'd still be in the poky, and in there for keeps no doubt.

It's all a matter of record how the poxy inquiry turned out. It was all very well done though, you have to give them that. When I eventually had my turn in the box they came out with all these photos of me like atop this statue and waving my arms and giving the fisted salute and all that like I was urging on the troops, and it doesn't matter that I know I didn't do that, that I spent the whole time like holding on for dear life to this statued guy's neck with my legs wrapped about his chest. No, that's not the point, 'cos after like two days of watching the video clip and studying the pictures and listening to this mental soundtrack, it's like even I was starting to think that maybe I did do all that incitement stuff and somehow forgot it all with the sheer excitement. They eventually had to say not-proven to my murdering Joanne, but gave me ten years for my part in the George riot and associated deaths.

Maybe sounds strange, but it was like a relief to get into the jail what with the fucking inquiry thing lasting eight months and the trial another five, and it was like every day we were getting herded in like a bunch of sad cows and the deep fustiness of the place was pure nose-assault every day, dusty and dry and stinking of old books. Emma put up a bit of a scrap, tried to tell it like it was, but there wasn't a shred of evidence to back up her conspiracy theory, and my hard-disc was completely empty even though the defence managed to dig up a data distribution list from the council records that showed Joanne had downloaded a mass of material to me on the afternoon of her murder.

There's no way I was taking the blame for Joanne, and that was the only time during the trial I really stood up and tried to make a fist of it, but they had enough witnesses – Bobby, Kieran, even Danny were all lined up and were trotted in to back up their written statements that it was me. Of course, I likewise signed a whole

stack of like pure confessions and sightings and totally
detailed statements about Shuggs being my closest
friend in the Shaws, and I even had Penny as the one
who slashed Kelly. Kelly turned up and had her day and
was like going to town on me, saying I was always
giving them whammers and yelloids and such as if it
was just like of-a-morning sort of thing, and making
out like I was into leading my little ladies astray and
debauching them and all that. So pretty soon you can
imagine that we're all being held up as like pure figures
of hate and even inside we were taking pelters from
other captives every chance they got so that confine-
ment of the solitary variety was demanded by all.

One of the papers even had a picture of Mum on the
front page and it said Terrorist's Tart Mum Exposed
and was all on about Mum and Guy and this escort
business they were trying to run, but it surely couldn't
have lasted long after that, even if such a thing existed,
though I've never been in touch with her since so don't
know for sure. And even the jewellery I bought her, that
got brought in as evidence of proceeds of crime which
was like how I was supposed to have raised funds for
the Shaws' terrorist activities.

None of the heid-bummer rozzloiders even turned up
on account of them all having retired and not bound to
appear, but they did send in statements all about how
beastly and subversive an organisation the Shaws was
and how it had been planning social unrest for years
and so on. It turns out that I was working for the Shaws
and my title was Commissioner's Office Infiltration
Co-ordinator, one of many functions I performed in the
organisation, all on record, right down to my wages
and all that.

There was days of testimony from these like pure desk-bound suits, all experts on this and that, information technology, industrial espionage, you name it, and they all like chorused this idea that the Shaws was a truly fearsome underground movement in the pay of foreign despots, and ready to bring chaos and unrest on a grand scale. And I was one of their senior staff, way up in the whole set-up, a real decision-maker, and you could see the jury getting to hate me more and more with every day that passed.

I was one of the first to go down. Emma got twenty-five years but hung herself before she was due to be transferred to Wimslow Hall. Danny got three years, but that was suspended on account of her being so ill. Kelly got seven years, and was pretty lucky given that various statements, including one of mine, had named her as Gerry's killer. Another thirty or so Shaws got stuck away, and three of them committed suicide awaiting trial. No rozz faced charges, and fourteen who were in the George that day claimed for psychological damage and got undisclosed compensation.

The wannabees get bigger and stronger but younger. Changed days indeed. Changed days from when it was yours truly who strode down the road with her little ladies and feeling pretty invincible and rather chuffed what with being our own bosses and working as and when we wanted and not being answerable to anyone. It was a good time I think now, and I felt free. I've still got some of the pictures from the papers, the one with me atop the horse, and the other showing me and my little ladies sauntering bold as you like down the road outside the Maggie. You can't really make out our faces that well but you'd know it was us if you knew us at all.

Now, maybe I'm free-er, I don't know. I'm staying with this guy, Kevin. He's alright. Bevs too much and gets a wee bit physical now and then but I just slap him good-style and a crack on the ear is usually enough to make him shut it. I think he actually likes it, truth be told. But outside the flat I have to be very careful. The wee local teams are hard enough, but there's super squads who come a-roaming now and then, and most unpleasant they are too, having no official control over them and usually well in with local top-rozz. They are sort of Vikings I suppose, moving across the city from area to area on something like a seasonal basis and plundering as they go. But they're the main distributors for most naughtiness and have to be dealt with, so I always end up paying well over the odds for whatever I get, not prepared any more to deal face to face with these nerrdowells. I've had enough of scrapping. The eyesight is really quite bad now and you can't go fisticuffing with great big gregs on.

I hardly ever get my hands on gear as good as what they put me on during the inquiry and the trial, but I get my script from the chemmy and it's usually enough to see me by until the weekend. Kevin doesn't like me taking guys back, but I only ever use the spare room and he's always knocked out with booze anyway so I don't know what the problem is. I won't usually do it unless we've bills that really won't wait any longer, and if they don't cough up I'll end up robbing them anyway, so a couple of nights can get me two or three ton easy.

Proper work comes in dribs and drabs. I'm with the security agency that covers the big festivals and such-like, and it's busy Summertime. But I'm getting a bit slow for it now and this year was pretty bad, got a real tanking down at the Waterfront one night, that's how my nose got like this. And the scar is from a stint I had at the Mercury. What a hole that is. So I suppose I've lost some of my symmetrical prettiness of late. Not that he minds, or says anyroad, but laughable it would be if he did, given that he looks like death warmed up. I've been trying to get back into the exercise, and I even got a totty-sack and filled it half-way with sand and put a bit of cord on it but there's no room in this place to hang a bag and even if there was I can't practise kicking 'cos of the noise, and that bastard underneath isn't shy about bringing his snarly hounds up to bark at the door if I overstep it noise-wise in any regard.

I still think about Joanne. Every single night, usually when I'm trying to get to sleep and hearing the screams of the George that day and the horribleness of those poor bastards being trampled to death. At least I never got trampled, and neither did Joanne, but I still remember the wee man with the red blotches, and the smell of his hair is tied in with the screams and the silence afterwards and I'll never ever forget it.

Sometimes I dream that I pick up the phone one day and Joanne's there, and I don't hear her voice but I get the buzzing and grinding of an E-message, and all this stuff pours out the phone, sheets and sheets of ribbony thin paper linked together, miles of it, about how we were all used and chucked away when they were done with us, and it's all dry as dust, names and times and numbers, but it's the truth and it's nowhere to be found except in the noggins of those who were there that day. And even though I know when I pick up the phone in the dreams it's Joanne who's there, and even though she doesn't speak, I wish she would leave me alone now. It's as if she thinks I'm still trying to find out the truth so she's still trying to send it to me. But I'm not looking any more, and wish she would stop. Maybe the one thing I've found out, and one thing we never really talked about that much, is how dangerous it is to try and punch over your weight. I won't be doing it again in a hurry.

Maybe it was me right enough. My fault she did what she did, my fault she thought she could fight anyone, even the rozz and the suits. My fault she got knifed and died alone.

I believe it was Bobby who stuck the knife in Joanne. That's the job he was given, and he did it. I did mine. Joanne was doing hers. Who's to say who was in the right or the wrong? Certainly not me, given that I'm a terrorist and an enemy of the state and the people and all that. And as far as anyone who reads the papers or watches the box is concerned, it was me who did her anyway.

But I suppose she must have really known I was her friend if she tried to get the stuff to me. She must still have trusted me, even if I was working for the bastards. So that makes me feel better.

I've been toying with the idea of starting up another team. We wouldn't get taken on by the Commissioner's Office, but there's plenty of freelance stuff in the small business side of things. It's pretty hairy, but the dosh is good, and if you can last even six months you can make enough to get yourself a one-roomer in Spain for a year, just take off and do some relaxing and smoking and remembering.

I call Danny every now and then, but I have to keep it very short 'cos I know they'll have her well tapped. She still can't talk, but her Mum kind of listens on the other line and translates for her as she moans and grunts. Whatever they gave her during the trial caused an embolism and she ended up having a big chunk of brain-meat cut out.

Josie's still with the Shaws. They're all split up now since being declared illegal. But it seems like they're still battering away, joining camps here and there, indulging in the ancient sport of rozz-bashing as and when they get the chance, and the last I heard big Maxo was being hunted for inciting trouble at some road protest down South. Shuggs managed to disappear completely. Bobby, as far as I know, might still be with the Commissioner's Office Operations Control, but there's no way of tracing whereabouts he is, and Robert Harris wasn't his real name anyway. I've given up imagining what to do to him. It just eats away at you.

So tonight's a normal Wednesday. Kev'll be down in The Vaults with his sap cronies, jarring and smoking and making up excuses as to the whereabouts of his cheque proceeds. I'll get this place squared up and then finish off the last of the syrup. The telly's not bad. Couple of those new mushroom folded pizzas. I can't get enough of them right now. Hopefully he'll go up to the pool hall with his mates after closing time and I'll get some peace.

I managed to chuck the fags as soon as I found out I was pregnant, but just the occasional toot can't do much harm. I haven't picked any names yet, even though they've already told me to expect a boy. Not Kevin anyway. Just a pity it's not a girl, 'cos then I'm sure I know what I'd call her.

Well, sort of sure.